CLEAN HOLIDAY ROMANCE COLLECTION

Mistletoe Magic

DAISY LANDISH

First Edition
ISBN ebook: 978-1-998178-21-6
ISBN paperback: 978-1-998178-20-9

Editing by Rachael Lammie
Cover by Daisy Landish

BEACHES AND TRAILS
PUBLISHING

ABOUT THE AUTHOR

Daisy Landish is a romance and contemporary fiction author living in the UK, whose clean and sweet novellas have tugged at readers' heart-strings across the pond and beyond. When she's not writing love stories, Daisy spends her time reading, hiking at dawn, and riding into the sunset on her horse, Rosebud.

www.daisylandishromance.com

facebook.com/daisylandishromance

twitter.com/daisy_landish

instagram.com/beachesandtrailspublishing

amazon.com/author/daisylandish

bookbub.com/authors/daisy-landish

goodreads.com/Daisy_Landish

ALSO BY DAISY LANDISH

Clean Regency Romance

The Lady Series - The Allington Collection

The Lady Series - The Gillingham Collection

The Lady Series - The Blackmore Collection

Clean Contemporary Romance

Love on Spruce Island

Second Chance

Cherry Tree Island

The Wedding Trio

The Science Fair Trilogy

Clean Contemporary Western Romance

Counting on a Cowboy

Focusing on the Cowboy

Cozy Mysteries

Jane and Kennedy Daniels Mysteries

Pine Grove Mysteries

Annie Archer Paranormal Mysteries

Wilma Wade Holiday Mysteries

Mike and Maddie Mysteries

Clean Holiday Romance

The Yuletide Thief

Grounded at Christmas

Clueless at Christmas

Christmas Surprise

A HOLIDAY ROMANCE

Clueless at Christmas

DAISY LANDISH

CHAPTER 1
EMILY

would feel much happier knowing you were flying here. The thought of you driving all that way alone worries me," Mom complained into the phone. "If you're worried about the cost, I'll pay for the flight myself. It's no trouble to have my little girl with us at Christmas." I could hear her smile through the phone.

"Mom, I'm not a little girl. I'm twenty-three. It's only a four-hour drive, I'll be fine. I'll be home in time for dinner on Christmas Eve. Stop worrying." I laughed, hearing her sigh in frustration.

She knew how stubborn I could be. It was a trait I inherited from her. We talked for a little longer before I had to go. I still had to pack and wrap my gifts.

The next morning, I tossed my bag and gifts into the back of my little silver Volkswagen Beetle, cranked up the radio, and started my trip from San Francisco to the small mountain town of Graeagle, about sixty miles outside of Reno.

As soon as I turned eighteen, I moved to San Francisco. Though it upset my parents, I just could not stay living in a town where everyone knew everything about everyone. Daddy always said my dreams were bigger than Graeagle, and as always, he was right.

I watched the city go by and slowly vanish in my rear-view mirror. Concrete buildings gave way to rows of snow-covered trees.

I turned up the radio a little louder and sang along with Leanne Rimes as home drew closer. I loved living in the city, and I never once doubted my decision to move. Still, nothing beat the moment the city was left behind, and the country landscape and mountain air waved hello. The landscape around me turned from green to white as the snow started falling thicker and harder. The music stopped, and a cheerful voice chimed over the radio.

"We interrupt our regularly scheduled programming to bring you an important weather update. Blitzen, the festive storm will likely hit Sacramento, Reno and travel up through northern California in the next few hours. Expect high winds upwards of fifty miles an hour, below zero temperatures, and heavy snowfall. It looks like it will be a white Christmas after all, as the storm is reported to be here for the rest of the week. So, stay safe out there people. If you are traveling home for Christmas, we advise a quick journey as the roads will get icy very soon. Now let's get the Christmas spirit flowing. The next song is Baby It's Cold Outside by Dean Martin."

Winter in Graeagle was cold enough without the prospect of a winter storm. The trees zoomed by as fast as other cars traveling back down toward San Francisco. As the day wore on, the darkness only made it harder to see through the blizzard. The radio started breaking up as interference from the storm distorted the signal. The constant crackle was messing with my head, and I turned it off. It was taking everything I had to stay focused and calm as I made my way up the mountains through the sheet of white now covering my windshield. The snow was piling on faster than the wipers could clear it.

I saw the bridge I needed to cross to start the long drive up toward home. That bridge meant that I had already covered half of my journey. My phone rang. I glanced to the passenger seat where my phone sat and saw 'Mom' flash on my screen.

"Ironic, Mom. Considering you say you don't want me answering my phone while driving, and you know I'm driving right now," I yelled at the phone, struggling to control my car. I could feel the tires slipping on the road. My phone rang again. "I'll call you back," I yelled at my phone as if Mom could hear me without picking up the call.

I don't know why bridges are more slippery than roads. I should look it up sometime. But now, I debated whether I should pull over and call Mom back when I got to the other side.

Though I drove as carefully as I could, my tires slid over the black ice. And though I knew better, fear made me slam on the breaks.

I watched in horror as my car started spinning in slow motion. Before I could blink or breathe, the front of the car smashed into a tree while the back broke the guardrail of the bridge. I hit my head on the steering wheel on impact. Though the car could go no further, it was still moving. Maybe I had a concussion and only felt like it was moving. I checked my rear-view mirror for oncoming traffic and my heart stopped. The back of my car was teetering over the edge of the bridge. Though the river was narrow and likely frozen, I did not want to drop the twenty or so feet.

If I go down with the car, I could die. I needed to get out of the car. I took off my seat belt and unlocked the door. I was the heaviest thing in the car; I was keeping it from falling. I had to quickly open the door and get out or I'd get hit by the door and pulled down with the car. I took a deep breath and moved my feet closer to the door, turning my body slowly as I did.

Good, my legs aren't broken.

I moved my fingers and tested my wrist. All clear. Shoulders? Fine. I put one hand on the handle and squeezed it, pushing the door only enough for it to unlatch. So far so good. Another deep inhale, and I pushed the door with both hands and leaped out, angling left and throwing myself on the ground to avoid the car door slamming into me. It worked. I was out.

———

I don't know how long I lay in the snow. When I woke, I was so cold I thought I might have hypothermia. There was blood in the snow where I'd passed out. I raised a hand to my head and found a cut over my right eyebrow. It wasn't bleeding at the moment; the cold snow had likely staunched the flow.

I knelt and checked for other injuries. Finding none, I pulled myself to my feet. The wind was fierce, blowing my hair around my face. My head began to throb. I pulled on the hood of my jacket and scolded myself for not following Mom's advice of wearing a full-size parka when I came to the country.

The compact fleece usually did the trick, but it only covered my torso. My skinny jeans were caked in snow and my ankle boots were no match for the knee-high snow on the road.

I reached in my pocket for my phone, only to remember that it was in the cup holder. In the car. At the bottom of the ravine. Tears welled up in my eyes. If I didn't die of frostbite, Mom would kill me for sure.

I stuffed my hands in my pockets and started walking. It was Christmas Eve, people were going to be home, especially during a blizzard. I started walking.

I walked for a long time before I saw signs of life. I could barely feel my toes and the tip of my nose felt like it might fall off if I touched it. Once, after I'd tripped and fallen face-first in the snow, I wondered if I should just curl up on the side of the road and wait for death to take me.

Scanning the horizon, I breathed a sigh of relief when I saw smoke peeking out over the trees. Though I couldn't see the house it came from, it gave me hope. I got up and pressed on.

CHAPTER 2
JACOB

made it home from work just before the storm hit. The weather outside had become monstrous. I couldn't remember a storm this bad since I'd moved out here. It was all over the news at the hospital and on the radio on the drive home. It seemed even the weatherwoman underestimated the magnitude of this storm.

Storm Blitzen. Who names these storms?

I tossed a few more logs on the fire and started checking my supplies. If there was a power outage, I wanted to be ready. I got some candles, flashlights, extra blankets, and some bottled water I kept for emergencies out of the storage closet.

I put my coat on and went to get more firewood from the pile outback. I set the shovel near the door in case I needed to go back again before it was time to go back to work.

I crouched near the fireplace, rubbing my hands together and trying my best to get some heat in my bones. It was brutal out there.

Next, I checked the TV. I had shelled out the extra bucks to get satellite reception, but when snowfall was this heavy, it was likely out.

Yep. That means no internet and probably no cell reception either.

I checked my phone and sighed. I had been looking forward to unwinding and watching the shows that had been piling up in my recorder. I'd been working for six days straight.

"Well, I guess I'll just read a book," I said to my empty cabin.

I headed to the kitchen and started dinner. My stomach growled like a bear, a side effect of working as an E.R. doctor is you had, no breaks for lunch or even snacks. I was famished.

The steak was just starting to sizzle nicely when I heard a knock at the door. My cabin was, by design, out in the middle of nowhere. I liked my privacy. My work at a big hospital in Reno was hectic and I appreciated the peace and quiet that came with being in the lone cabin at the end of a hidden drive. No one came here by chance. They were either invited, lost, or trouble. I glanced at the shotgun hidden in the coat rack by the door, always loaded, ready for an emergency. Thankfully, I had never had to use it, but it was nice to have it there. It gave me peace of mind.

I turned off the stove and headed to the door.

"Who's there?" I asked with my deepest, most threatening voice. I stood listening, hoping for some kind of indication as to what or who was outside. It might be the wind, or a bear. I heard a squeak that sounded oddly like a woman's voice. I flung the door open, and on my porch stood a half-frozen young woman. I stood, longer than I should, just looking at her. She was a mess. I checked behind her and saw no car. Had she walked here? From where?

Her forehead had a nasty-looking cut that stretched from just above her right eye into her hairline, caked blood running down her face. I went into doctor mode.

"You're bleeding. Come in, I can help you," I said.

Though she was clearly frozen and about to faint, she gave me a once over, assessing whether or not I might be a serial killer. "Are you alone, here?" she asked with a barely audible voice. She was weak as a kitten.

I raised my one visible hand and I let go of the gun I held with the other behind the door, reaching instead for my lanyard in my coat pocket. I held it up for her to see. "I'm alone. But I'm also a doctor. I can help. You can trust me." I spoke slowly so as not to spook her.

She squinted at the swaying ID in front of her. Deciding it was legit, she grabbed it and placed it in her pocket. I let her.

"Can I use your phone?" she asked, leaning on the door jamb.

"I'm sorry the phones are down and there's no cell service this far out.," I said, reaching for my phone to show her. She gave it a cursory glance and hung her head in defeat.

"Come inside, honey," I said, gently taking her arm and pulling her in. I closed the door behind her and walked her to the couch. I had to press her shoulders down so she would sit. She was staring at the fire. "Give me a minute, I'll get you something to drink."

I went to the kitchen and put the kettle on. I grabbed one of the water bottles, opened the cap, and took it to her. "Drink," I ordered. She took a tentative sip, then seemed to register it was water and she that was parched and started downing the bottle. Good.

I went to my room to get my medical bag. When I got back, she hadn't moved, but she'd finished the bottle.

"I'm a doctor; you don't need to be so scared. I need to clean that cut before it gets infected," I said.

She seemed to be thawing out but hadn't taken off her coat. Her eyes kept darting to the door like she might bolt as soon as she was warm enough. I put my bag on the floor in front of her and went to the kitchen to get her a hot drink. It would warm her hands and give her something to do.

When I came back, she hadn't moved. I handed her the mug.

"I hope you like herbal tea. Chamomile is soothing," I said, and she took a tentative sip.

"What happened?" I asked, taking the things I'd need and placing them on the coffee table. I pulled on a pair of surgical gloves and put some disinfectant on a piece of gauze, holding them out in front of her and waiting for consent. She nodded and I started to wipe the blood off her face.

"The bridge was icy. I crashed my car in the tree and the car went over the railing," she said flatly, devoid of any emotion.

"You walked here in a blizzard from the bridge?" I asked, keeping my tone as neutral as I could manage. Any other girl would be hysterical by now. She was either super stoic or in shock. It had to be the latter.

"Yeah, is it far?" she asked, her voice still monotone.

"About five miles," I said. I'd cleaned up her face and the wound. She wouldn't need stitches. A little surgical tape and she'd have a hairline scar for her trouble. I took off my gloves and announced, "All done."

Her fingers flew to the site in wonder. "That was fast, thanks."

"It was a smaller cut than I thought. You didn't need stitches, but you might have a small scar," I said, grimacing in apology.

She shrugged. "I think I'm lucky to be alive."

While that was certainly true, it was time to lighten the mood. I stuck out my hand.

"Dr. Sanborn, but you can call me Jake."

She smiled and took my hand.

"Nice to meet you, Jake. I'm…" she trailed off as a frown came over her face.

I waited, keeping my face neutral. It wasn't uncommon for people to get short-term memory loss after a head injury or major trauma.

Her face flooded with alarm and tears sprang to her eyes. Though there was nothing Jacob hated worse than crying females, emotions were a step up in this situation.

"I. I can't remember my name," she said, her lip was quivering, and she was looking around the room wildly as if there might be a clue hidden in the cabin.

"Don't panic. You hit your head and you've been through a traumatic experience. These things happen. It's only temporary, try to relax," I replied, tone soothing and calm.

"Drink up your tea, it'll warm you up," I added.

She looked at me, then and her eyes widened as if she was only just realizing I was there. "You're a doctor," she said. I nodded. She took a long sip of her tea and pulled my hospital badge out of her pocket. "Doctor Jacab Sanborn," she read, holding up the picture next to my face. "Is that your medical opinion or are you trying to keep me calm so I don't freak out?" she asked.

"Both," I said honestly. I wouldn't lie to her. There was no telling with these things.

"In 85% of similar cases, patients regain their memory in less than forty-eight hours."

She nodded at this and gave me back my badge. "And the other 15%?"

"Those are usually complex cases or people who had a predisposition or suffered more severe injuries," I said.

"So, what is your prescription, doctor?" she asked. The color was creeping back into her face.

"You should relax. Try to stay calm and focus on the positive. You're safe, mostly uninjured, and you've found a warm place to wait out the storm." I said and got up.

"I don't know about you, but I'm starving. How about some dinner?" I asked.

CHAPTER 3
EMILY

As soon as he mentioned, food I found that I was starving too. The guy seemed legit, and he had an excellent bedside manner. They must love him at the hospital. It didn't hurt that he was handsome, tall, and built like a linebacker.

He looked like he was older than me by a few years. Maybe thirty? With the frame he had, I wondered if perhaps he'd gone through med school while in the military. He had the shape and the haircut. But he seemed too gentle to be a soldier.

He had the kind of deep brown eyes a girl could get lost in. And the five o'clock shadow on his chiseled jaw was sexy as hell. While my instincts told me to beware of mountain men, my hormones were screaming at me to stay.

"Sure, I could eat," I replied as coolly as I could.

"I'll get dinner going. Why don't you take a hot shower and get out of those wet clothes?"

When I crossed my arms and eyed him suspiciously, he added, "I have a spare bedroom. You can change in there, and I'll give you some dry clothes."

Reluctantly, I got up and handed him the cup. I shrugged out of my wet coat and stood there wondering what to do next. He took it and put it on the coat rack by the door. He nodded for me to follow. He pointed out his room, the bathroom, and the spare bedroom.

"I'll get you a towel," he said and came back with a fluffy towel, a grey tracksuit with a college football logo, and a pair of thick wool socks.

"I'll be in the kitchen," he said, pointing to the other end of the cabin and backing up as if he'd just deactivated a bomb.

"Thanks," I said. "For everything."

"Don't mention it," he said and left.

The warmth of the shower was exactly what I needed. I could feel the tension in my aching muscles melt away like butter on a warm bagel.

After my shower, I dressed in the clothes he gave me. I felt like a kid wearing her dad's clothes. They were too big, but the pants had a drawstring, and I managed to keep them up. The hoodie had so much material that I didn't feel so awkward about not wearing a bra. I washed my clothes in the sink and hung them in the room. They'd be dry in the morning.

When I joined him in the kitchen, he'd laid out two huge plates of food: Steak, roasted veggies, and a salad. Hungry as I was, there was no way I'd get through all of that.

"Hungry?" he asked.

"Like a bear," I said, and we both started laughing. We sat down and started to eat.

"The storm outside looks like it's getting worse. I'm sure it'll ease up by morning. Once the roads are clear, we can head out and hunt for your car. Sound good?" he said, not looking up from his plate, which he tore at like a hungry lion. I nodded and let out a little chuckle that finally made him look up at me. He sat back a second as if seeing me for the first time, almost like he had forgotten I was here.

"What's so funny?" he asked, tucking back into his food.

"Just the way you're attacking your plate," I laughed, trying not to attack mine the same way. The steak was so tender I could almost cut it with my fork.

"Oh, no," he said. "Are you a vegetarian?" he asked with a pained expression, pointing at my half-finished plate.

I burst out laughing. "No, not at all. "I'm a meat-eater, through and through," I replied. "That's just way too big a portion for me."

"Are you sure?" he asked, eyeing me and the food on my plate. I pushed it toward him with a nod. He took it and added the food to his plate. I tried not to laugh.

"I'm sure. You're an amazing cook." Without a second thought, I added, "Good looking, a doctor, and a chef, will you marry me?" I froze in horror. A slow smile spread over his face as he stopped chewing and looked at me.

"Oh my god. I can't believe I just said that" I blurted, covering my face with my hands. Jake chuckled but didn't comment. He resumed eating, and all I wanted was for the floor to open up and swallow me.

CHAPTER 4
JACOB

didn't get too excited by her comment at dinner. Don't get me wrong, even in my ugly sweats, the girl was hot. But she also had a head injury and didn't even remember her own name. She may be behaving out of character. Besides, she was clearly mortified. It was best to let it go.

I made coffee and brought out the fruit cake I'd gotten from the supermarket. She asked about my job. While didn't normally talk about work outside of work, she seemed grateful for the change of topic. I told her about med school and my career up until now, keeping it light.

We made the dishes and I asked if she wanted to watch a movie, but she begged off and headed for bed. I checked her vitals and cleared her for bed. She didn't seem to have a concussion or a temperature. Nothing a hot shower, a home-cooked meal, and a good night's sleep wouldn't cure.

I gave her a toothbrush, a bottle of water, and a flashlight. "In case the power goes out during the night," I explained. She gave me a timid smile and said goodnight.

———

The next day, the storm was still going and there had to be at least four feet of snow outside. I woke up, made coffee, and went outside to fetch more wood. It was still freezing out there.

I didn't know what she liked for breakfast, or even if she ate in the morning, so I made everything. It was Christmas after all. I made blueberry pancakes, scrambled some eggs, bacon, and roasted potatoes. It was a feast, and I was dying for her to get up so we could eat.

I had a bagel while I waited and opened the latest John Grisham novel that I never got around to reading.

When she finally came out of the spare bedroom at nine, she was wearing her own clothes again and had put her hair up in a ponytail. After using the bathroom, she came into the kitchen and laughed at the spread on the table.

"Wow! Do you always eat like this?" she asked waving at the food.

"No, I usually have no time to eat. So, when I'm home, I make up for lost time," I said. I got up and put my book on the counter, face down because I didn't have a bookmark handy.

"Besides, it's Christmas," I announced.

Her face lit up for about a second and a half. God, she was beautiful. But it turned sad just as quick, and tears welled up in her eyes.

"Oh, honey, don't cry," I said moving closer to her. I stood there awkwardly, unsure of how to comfort her. I placed a hand in the middle of her back. That was safe. I made slow circles and she started to sob. Ugh.

"It's going to be okay. You'll see," I said in soothing tones. When she hiccupped, I gave up and pulled her into a hug. She didn't resist. I let her cry while I gently stroked her back and kept up a stream of reassuring words like, 'I know', 'it's okay', 'you're safe', and 'I've got you'.

Her hands were clutching my t-shirt and her forehead rested on my left peck. I wasn't crazy about the crying but hugging her felt really good. I couldn't remember the last time I'd held a woman. Don't get me wrong, I had sex on a regular basis. Doctors, nurses, and orderlies were the raunchiest bunch of misfits I'd ever seen. But like food, sleep, and rest, we took it on the go.

No, I mean holding a woman you cared about. Try as I might, I couldn't recall anyone I'd cared enough about to comfort other than my mom and she'd been gone for over a decade. Both my parents died in a car accident, a head-on collision with a drunk driver. It's what had prompted me to become an E.R. doctor. They hadn't died on impact, they'd died of complications while in the emergency room.

The girl wasn't shaking anymore, and her breathing was evening out. Though the storm outside still raged, it seemed the one inside her was abating.

I loosened my arms and let her walk out of them.

"Thanks," she said. "I needed that." I grabbed the box of Kleenex from the counter and gave it to her. She blew her nose and wiped her eyes.

"I'm sorry about your shirt," she said, pointing at the wet spot her tears had made.

Without thinking I took it off. She went stock still, her eyes huge.

It was hard to tell if she was shocked that I was half-naked or impressed by my toned physique. Either way, I didn't want to embarrass her or make her uncomfortable, so I fled the room mumbling about getting a fresh t-shirt.

A day with a beautiful woman whose name I did not even know. We had a lovely Christmas Day, nonetheless. We cracked open a bottle of wine, ate good food, and talked about everything and nothing. I found I spent most of the time just watching her. She was mesmerizing.

Three days had gone by since her arrival, and the storm was still going strong, leaving us snowed in. Not knowing her name made conversation a little awkward. So as a joke, I nicknamed her Rapunzel because her hair was long, thick, and chestnut with sunkist highlights. I had to laugh at how it annoyed her. She would cross her arms and give me a stern look telling me to stop it, but it just made me stick with it. She was beautiful. Even in my baggy clothes, I could tell her body was trim and toned. Her eyes, so deep, sparkled when she laughed. It was getting increasingly harder to hide my attraction to her.

By day four, her memories had started to come back. She remembered she lived in San Francisco and worked at a fashion magazine, but the name was still unknown, as was her own. She recalled her family lived in Graeagle, which was a town not so far away. The fact that she lived all but a day's drive or a short flight away gave me hope that when she could eventually go home, we might see each other again. I enjoyed her company and found I was flirting a lot, which was something I never did. Once you get your heart broken as spectacularly as I had, you give up on women. But somehow, she was different. She inspired hope in me. Hope I thought I lost a long time ago. On day five, the storm had stopped. But the snow it left behind was still too thick to drive in. I noticed the firewood was running a little low, so I headed out back to chop some more. I must have woken her up because, by the time I worked up a sweat and looked up, I saw her standing at the back door, watching me intently with a lust-filled look on her face. "Hi there, enjoying the view?" I asked, winking back, flustered; she straightened up and scurried back inside.

CHAPTER 5
EMILY

was feeling mildly embarrassed about sobbing in the arms of a stranger on Christmas Day. But when he took off his shirt, I was shocked back to reality. Up until that point, he was just Doctor Nice Guy. The patient, caring, Samaritan who'd taken in a stray dog, fed it, and gave it a warm bed for the night.

This guy? He was calendar hot. I could just imagine him in his low-hung blue jeans swinging an ax and splitting logs. I couldn't get the image out of my mind, and I couldn't stop staring at him. I must have scared him because he fled the room like he was being chased by bandits. It gave me time to collect myself. I splashed cold water on my face from the kitchen sink. As much to wash away the puffiness from the tears as to cool myself off. Down girl.

When he came back, he had on an identical t-shirt, but he'd added a red plaid shirt over top, buttoned up.

Oh, god. He's afraid of me, now.

"Hungry?" he asked.

I knew he meant the food, but just then I'd have taken a few servings of him.

"Yes! This looks amazing!" I said with more cheer than I felt.

We had breakfast and he asked what he should call me.

It didn't spur a memory and I was stumped.

"You decide," I replied.

He put his fork down and sat back in his chair, eyeing me up. He crossed his arms and cupped his chin in his hand. He was putting a lot of thought into this.

"We could go the easy route and call you Jane. You know, like Jane Doe," he started.

I shook my head. Not because I didn't like it, but because I was enjoying the game.

"With your curly chestnut hair, and those big brown eyes, I'm going to call you Julia," he stated.

"Julia? Why Julia?" I asked.

"Because you remind me of Julia Roberts," he said.

"But she's gorgeous!' I replied.

"Yeah," he said nodding his head. He made eye contact and I blushed. He was flirting with me!

"Come on, let's get the dishes done and then we'll see if you're any good at Scrabble," he said, getting up and gathering up some of the plates.

Hours later we were fighting like an old married couple over some sketchy words he'd put on the board. He claimed they were in Latin and that it was allowed. I begged to differ and soon we gave up playing because he was hungry again.

"Is it lunchtime already?" I asked as we put the game away.

"Yup!" he said gleefully. I had to laugh. He was adorable.

"How about tomato soup and some grilled cheese sandwiches?" he asked.

"Sounds good. Can I help? I feel bad, you keep doing all the work," she said following him into the kitchen.

"There's not much to do. If you want, you can make dinner later," he suggested.

"That's a great idea!' I said and felt better now that I knew I'd be pulling my own weight.

After lunch, I told him to go ahead and read his book. I checked his bookcase and found one that looked good, but I ended up having a long nap instead.

———

That night, I made spaghetti Bolognese. I found the recipe in a book in his kitchen, and he was polite enough to act like he was enjoying it, but I'm no fool. It tasted awful. Clearly, I was not a chef. The fact he choked it down and didn't say a word was a testament to what a nice guy he was. Fortunately, my salad and garlic bread were delicious, as was the wine he'd poured for us. The brownies I made were a bit over-done, but with a little hot fudge sauce and a scoop of vanilla ice cream, they were fine.

He asked if I wanted a glass of brandy and I declined. The wine had gone straight to my head, and I figured I should keep my wits about me lest I jump his bones in my inebriated state.

"How about a movie?" he asked.

"That's a great idea? What are the options?" I asked and he pointed to the same bookcase where I'd found my book earlier. Most of the movies were action flicks, where things blow up, men go to war, or chase each other in fast cars. As it was Christmas, I chose Die Hard.

"Good choice," he replied, and set it up.

I sat down at the other end of the sofa and curled my feet under me.

"Aren't you going to sit a little closer?" he asked, raising his eyebrows. "I promise I don't bite. Well, not unless you ask me to."

I laughed and scooted closer to the middle. Jacob put his arm around me, and I leaned into him. It felt right. I noticed he was wearing cologne. I don't recall smelling it on him that morning. It was an intoxicating scent that woke up all my senses and made me want to get even closer to him.

At the end of the movie, I realized I had seen it before. Jacob said that was a good sign and that I should start remembering things soon.

"Are you tired?" he asked.

Though it was getting late, I didn't feel tired at all. Partly because of the nap I'd had, partly because I was super aware of the electricity that was going back and forth between us.

"Nope," I said. "You?"

He shook his head. "Let me check your wound," he said. I turned to face him. He lifted a corner of the bandage and peered at his handi-work. He pursed his lips and nodded his head. "Looks good. It might start to itch tomorrow. That a sign that it's healing up nicely."

"I had a great doctor," I replied as he replaced the bandage. When he was done, he rested one arm on the sofa, but the other one stayed on my face.

"You're even more beautiful than Julia Roberts," he said.

I closed my eyes and leaned my face into his hand, brushing my cheek against the rough skin of his thumb. When I opened them, he was closer. Much closer. I could feel the warmth of his breath on my face, lips inches away from kissing me, eyes boring into mine.

He was waiting for permission to kiss me. I surprised us both and kissed him. Softly at first, just a brush of the lips. He took over then. Pushing his hand through my hair and letting my hair out of the scrunchie.

With both hands, he held my head, fingers massaging my scalp as his mouth attacked mine with the same relish he had for food. He tasted, he sampled, he devoured. I never wanted this kiss to stop.

We let it run its course until we both had to come up for air.

"I think we should call it a night," he said, caressing my face and handing me my hair tie.

I didn't know if I should be glad or disappointed. That kiss was going places. But as I had only met this guy yesterday and I currently didn't even know my own name, I figured he was right.

CHAPTER 6
JACOB

That kiss was like nothing I had ever felt before. I was about to push her back against the sofa and find out if the rest of her tasted as good as those lips. Then I remembered she wasn't an intern, and I wasn't a rutting bull.

I got up and took a few steps back. I needed some distance. Though she didn't wear a ring, she might still have a spouse and a family. I'd feel like a heel if I took things further and she turned out to be another man's wife.

I stared at her, drinking in the sight of her. Memorizing every inch of her face, every contour. The way the light reflected off her hair. I wanted to enjoy this moment and make it last for as long as possible.

At some point, soon, the roads would be clear, her memories would come back, and she would leave. The thought tugged at my gut. I barely knew the girl, but already I knew I couldn't let her go.

I held my hand out to her and pulled her up.

"I'm so glad I got to spend Christmas with you," I whispered. She smiled; her eyes twinkled back at me. Those eyes. I swear I saw my future in those eyes. I really hoped she wasn't married. I was falling for her. I pulled her in and held her close. She wrapped her arms around my waist, and we stood there, both aware of the uncertainty that surrounded the budding feelings we were developing.

"I could hold you forever," I said, and I knew I spoke the truth. She squeezed me harder and replied, "I'd let you."

CHAPTER 7
EMILY

The next morning, I woke up feeling well-rested, elated, and still riding the high of last night. I felt like a giddy schoolgirl who had just kissed the lead football player of the school team. He was a complete gentleman, and I was glad we'd called it a night. It wouldn't have been right to let things go further when I had no idea if I was already in a relationship.

I walked to the bathroom and turned on the shower. Looking at my reflection, I looked to my lips, pressing my fingers to them gently, remembering the feel of his lips on mine. How could I feel so connected to a guy I'd only just met?

I showered and dressed in the tracksuit he'd lent me as my clothes weren't dry yet from washing them so late the night before. I was looking forward to another of those kisses.

But when I came out of the bathroom, the cabin was empty. I looked outside and saw his blue pickup truck was gone, and the roads were clear.

"He must have gone looking for my car," I said, closing the front door again as the cold rushed inside, biting at my face.

I headed to the kitchen and started making breakfast. I knew deep down that the little fairy tale bubble we were in was coming to an end.

When they found my car, they'd find my purse and ID. Even if I didn't remember, we'd have information to go on.

Placing two plates of bacon, eggs, and toast on the table, I heard the purr of an engine signaling he was home. I poured a cup of coffee and went to meet him at the door.

The door opened, and I could see a mix of joy and pain on his face. He wasn't alone. An older couple was with him. When I saw their faces, my heart exploded in my chest. I knew them. They were my parents. A huge grin split my face. I pushed the cup at Jake and ran to my parents. When he didn't catch it, the cup fell, sending coffee splashing across the floor. Memories flooded my mind. I started shaking as emotions overwhelmed me. All at once and much too quickly, memories washed over me like a tsunami.

"Mom, Dad," I breathed, as they held on to me for dear life.

"Emily, we were so worried. We filed a missing person's report and everything." My Mom sobbed in my ear, the smell of her floral perfume flooding my senses and wrapping around me like a comfort blanket. It reminded me of home. Emotions overwhelmed me and it all came back to me like a rushing tsunami. I held their faces, so happy to see them.

"I don't understand," I said, stepping back and looking to Jacob for answers. "How did you find me?"

"When I woke up, I saw that they had plowed the roads. I shoveled my way to the car and went to the bridge to check out the accident site and look for your purse. When I got there, I found a police cruiser, a tow truck, and an ambulance. I walked over to the officer and asked what was going on. Seeing the ambulance, I thought there might have been another accident. But he explained they hadn't found a body and pointed to the victim's family."

"He came over and asked us to describe our daughter," added Dad. "I thought that was odd, but I went along with it in case he might have seen you."

"Imagine our joy when he said he was pretty sure you were the girl that showed up at his cabin in the middle of the storm," put in Mom.

"They followed me back here and the rest, as they say, is history," finished Jacob.

"That's incredible," I replied and hugged them to me again.

My parents had coffee with Jacob while I changed. When it was time to go, I had mixed feelings. I was overjoyed at seeing my parents and regaining my memory. But at the same time, I already missed Jacob. We'd grown close and it felt like I was leaving a part of myself behind.

I don't know what he told my parents while I was changing, but they thanked Jacob and said they'd wait for me in the car while we said goodbye.

"So, Emily, it's nice to meet you," he said, extending his hand.

"It's nice to meet you too," I said, tugging on his hand to bring him closer. I grabbed hold of his shirt and pulled him down for a kiss.

"I guess that means you're not married," he asked with a smile.

"Totally single," I replied.

"Not anymore," he said before he kissed me.

The End.

Christmas Surprise

A CLEAN WESTERN HOLIDAY ROMANCE

DAISY LANDISH

CHAPTER 1

Christmas was Margo's favorite time of year. But, of course, it was her mother's favorite time of year too. Since her mother had passed, Margo did as her mother had done and went over the top with decorating. Every inch of her apartment was coated in something shimmery and covered in either fake snow or glitter. Walking into Margo's apartment was like entering a Christmas wonderland.

If the decorating wasn't enough, she even had a particular section of her closet filled with what she called 'festive wear.' Dresses in all shades of red and green, T-shirts adorned with snowflakes and reindeer, hats, scarves, everything you could think of for an array of occasions. She was prepared for everything from Christmas dinner with work colleagues to afternoons of Christmas shopping.

Margo subscribed to a music channel that played classic Christmas carols and the year's latest Christmas covers. She was sure – and proud to say – that she was likely the only person to have watched every Hallmark Holiday movie, some more than once.

Her favorite part was shopping. Not only did Margo love buying gifts for her loved ones, but she also loved people-watching. She loved sitting outside in the cold, wrapped up with a hot chocolate, watching couples kiss under the mistletoe, and excited children visiting the mall Santa. She loved decorations and carolers. All of it. Everywhere she looked, Margo could see magic. Christmas never lost its sparkle. Her skin would erupt into goosebumps. She lived for that magic chill.

Christmas shopping was an activity that Margo and her mother partook in every year. They would go gift shopping together and visit the independent vendor's stores for homemade cookies and soaps. After a long day of sharing the joy, they would sit outside – often in the snow – of the family-run coffee shop, Vanilla Latte, that kept the local Starbucks on their toes. Outside on the little silver chairs, they would huddle together with their hands wrapped around large cups of hot chocolate and listen to all the sounds of Christmas.

Even ten years after her mother's death, Margo never forgot the tradition and hoped to one day partake in it with her own children. She would sit, dreaming her mother was with her and imagining the conversations they would have. It was Margo's way of keeping her love of Christmas and her mother's memory alive.

She moved away from her family ranch, off to big city L.A., after her mother had died. Her mother had made Margo promise to follow her dreams. Margo's goal was to be a graphic designer, which was something she could do from any corner of the world. Her career gave her the freedom to travel. She loved the big city and kept her promise to her mother.

The first few years after her mother's death were rough. Margo had struggled with her father, who wanted her to run the family ranch with him, and she struggled even harder to gather the funds to move to L.A. But with her mother's words in her head and her memory in her heart, Margo powered through. She loved the hustle and bustle of Christmas shopping and the hunt for a bargain. So, with her treasures in hand, she headed home, looking forward to another Christmas in her wonderland apartment.

When she opened the front door, the red light on her answering machine flashed, indicating a message. Only one person left messages on her landline: her father. He never called her cell phone despite her telling him countless times.

"Hey darling, out shopping, I guess. Look, I want you to come and spend the holidays at the ranch. I miss you, and it's been too long since you have been home. Call me. It's Dad, by the way," said her dad's voice on the answering machine.

He always announced who he was at the end of his messages; it made her laugh. Unfortunately, her father was right. It had been far too many years since she had been home for the holidays, and her mother would be heartbroken.

Christmas at the ranch? How bad can it be? she thought as she called her father back and made the arrangements to head home.

CHAPTER 2

So, the infamous Margo Demorest was coming home for Christmas. Chase had acted like he was happy to hear the news, but he wasn't looking forward to it in the slightest. Chase and Margo had a history that he could forget and ignore when she was miles away in L.A., but not when she came home.

Chase and Margo had known each other since they were kids. They had basically faced every life lesson in front of each other, from kindergarten to when she left. But they had never got along. He had picked on her, and she had kicked and fought back. And when they were old enough to form their own opinions on life, they had opposing views. It was okay since they ran in different social circles. Still, everyone knew everyone's business living in the small ranch town of Grand Lake in Colorado.

When Margo's mother, Minnie, had passed after a long battle with cancer, Margo had gone a little off the rails, starkly contrasting to the put-together girl she used to be. Everyone knew Margo was battling with her father, and she did whatever she could to numb the pain. That's how Chase had bumped into her one night in a sketchy bar three towns over. Margo was drunk and had all kinds of unwanted male attention coming her way. When Chase intervened to make sure she was okay, it was his attention that caught her eye.

They had a hot and heavy, no-strings-attached fling that ended with no explanation when she up and left for L.A. Chase didn't care so much. It was what it was. It had confirmed his initial thoughts on Margo; she only cared about herself.

It had been years since she last came home, and the last visit hadn't been pleasant. Chase had suggested they pick up where they left off, and Margo slapped him across the face. She was even more enraged when her father told her he had hired Chase as a ranch hand.

"You can't be serious, Dad. Besides, he has no ranch hand experience," Margo had argued. She loved her father dearly, but some of his ideas were far-fetched, to say the least.

"How is one to get experience if no one gives you a chance? So, I'm giving him a chance," her father answered.

"But Dad."

"But Dad, nothing. You have made your feelings about the ranch very clear. It's my ranch. I am running it; therefore, I say who gets hired. If you don't like it, well, quite frankly, it's tough cookies."

Chase did not attempt to hide his satisfaction when Robert fought so hard for him. Margo was not so pleased. In thanks, Chase worked his backside off to make the ranch the best it could be. Robert had seen something in Chase that no one else had. None of his teachers believed in him; even his own father hadn't believed in him. Robert had believed in him, and Chase was determined to repay that belief with hard work.

Quickly, Chase rose the ranks to ranch manager, and the ranch had never been so successful. Soon after that, Chase had other ranchers trying to poach him. But Chase was loyal and believed in paying his debts. Robert had given him more than he could ever repay, and Chase wasn't going anywhere. So even when other ranchers offered a yearly salary three times what he was on, he had turned it down.

Chase worried for Robert. He hadn't been the same since Minnie's passing and Margo's departure. Chase thought he was giving up; the man seemed to be wasting away. However, Chase wanted to give the man something to live for and reignite his love for ranching. Even though Chase detested Margo, he hoped that her visit this holiday season would be what Robert needed.

CHAPTER 3

With her car packed full of gifts for her father and friends she missed the most, a box full of decorations – because she knew her dad wouldn't decorate the ranch – and a holiday playlist for the ride, Margo set off from L.A. to Colorado.

The drive was going to be fifteen hours. And since she still had some deadlines to hit, Margo decided to head up to the ranch two weeks before Christmas. She wanted to allow herself time to stop in Utah on the way and split the drive across two days but still have enough time to spend with her father before rushing back to L.A.

After a grueling eight-hour drive, Margo was exhausted and stopped at Green River, booking herself a night in a cozy little hotel with great reviews, views, and an indoor pool. After unpacking her car and settling into her room, she set up her laptop, finished a project, and submitted it via email before heading for a pre-dinner swim. Finally, after a delicious meal, she cozied up in bed with one of her favorite Hallmark Holiday movies, *A Heavenly Christmas*.

The following day, in full spirit, she packed her car and made the final part of her journey home. Her mind wandered as she drove, trying to enjoy the magic of her Christmas playlist. Was this going to be a pleasant holiday? Or was it yet another of her father's attempts to get her to take over the ranch? She worried about her father. He was overly attached to the ranch. And the last time she had visited, the ranch was barely making ends meet.

"Nope, I'm not going to think about it. It's Christmas. And nothing and no one is going to dampen my spirit," she said aloud, turning up the radio and continuing her drive.

———

Arriving at the ranch, Margo was exhausted and ready for a nap. Her breath caught at the rugged figure standing at the gates. Dark jeans, brown boots, a red plaid shirt, and a hat pulled down over his face. He had thick gloves on and hammered away, fixing an issue.

I wonder who this is, Margo thought as she pulled up the long driveway.

Hearing her car stop, the figure turned around and raised his head, finally bringing his face into view; chiseled features, cleanly shaven, with powder-blue eyes. She knew that face. And however handsome, it was a face she was not happy to see. From the look she received, the feeling was mutual. Chase Adams.

Great, just what I needed; he is still around, she thought as she drove past and onto her family's property.

Climbing out of her car, Margo realized that Chase had come closer. She wasn't in the mood and didn't have the energy to deal with him but decided to be as pleasant as possible to avoid a potentially awkward interaction.

"Chase, so good to see you. How have you been?" Margo asked, but even she could hear how fake her enthusiasm sounded.

Chase offered a knowing smile but decided to play along.

"Good to see you too; it's been too long. I'm doing great; how is life in the big city?" he asked, opening the trunk of her car and starting to unload.

"L.A. is amazing, everything I had hoped for....you don't need to unpack; I can handle it," she offered, grabbing the box of decorations from him.

"Sure you can," he chuckled sarcastically, his comment vexing Margo.

"Still the ever-chauvinistic pig I see. Some things never change," Margo rolled her eyes.

"Still got that childish attitude, I see. I guess things don't change," Chase fired back, causing Margo to shoot him an annoyed look.

"Change is the only constant in life," she retorted, storming off toward the house.

Chase followed swiftly behind with two of her boxes in hand.

"I said I don't want your help," Margo snapped, dropping her boxes in the hallway.

"No, you didn't. You said I didn't *need* to help. Wanting and needing are two different things."

Margo didn't know how to respond to that, looking dumbfounded and slightly annoyed at his self-satisfied face. Shoving his hands into his pockets and leaning against the door frame, Chase grinned at Margo.

"Look, I don't like you; you don't like me. That's a given, but we will have to find common ground while you are here. Your dad doesn't need us bickering."

Chase got under her skin, but she needed to calm down. The man had single-handedly pulled their ranch out of the hole her dad had dug. Furthermore, he was nice to her dad, and his very presence made it possible for her to have a life. She was grateful, but he didn't need to know that just yet.

"I agree," Margo nodded.

Chase offered his hand in a truce. Reluctantly, Margo shook it, surprised by how much she liked the feeling of his rough ranch hands on her skin.

"Now that's sorted, would you like help to your room with all these boxes?" Chase offered.

"That would be nice, thank you," Margo winced.

Silently, they walked up the stairs, and Margo was pleased to see her room was exactly how she had left it. Albeit there was an extra layer of dust from not being used. But she could clean that up in no time.

"I'll go grab you some clean bedding," Chase said, dropping the decorations on the bed.

"Wait, you know where the bedding is kept?" Margo asked, surprised.

"I should. I live here."

"What?!" Margo asked a little louder than she intended.

Chase laughed and went to the hallway, returning with fresh sheets and a new duvet set.

"Dinner should be served soon. See you later, Kitten," Chase said, tipping his hat before leaving.

'Kitten' was a nickname from school, a nickname she hated, and he knew it. Slowly, Margo felt herself losing her enthusiasm for spending the holidays at home. Now, all she wanted was to go back to L.A. as soon as possible. Swiftly changing her bedding and unpacking her things, she went out to search for her father.

She searched the house but couldn't find her father anywhere. As she went from room to room, she was flooded with memories of the happy life they'd shared before her dad started grooming her for a takeover. To her surprise, the place looked great, better than the last time she had visited. She popped into the kitchen to see her father helping Mrs. Morris with the cooking. Mrs. Morris had been the ranch cook ever since her mom passed. She was wonderful, like a grandmother figure to Margo and all the ranch staff loved her.

"Hey, Dad," Margo smiled.

"Darling, so good to see you. When did you get here?" he cheered, cleaning his hands before wrapping his arms around her.

Her father was thinner than she would like, but his skin had a healthy glow, and his eyes were bright. He looked happy. Even if she still worried about his health and mental wellbeing, Margo couldn't deny that he looked better than she had seen him in a long time, even with the extra grey hair in his beard and around his ears.

"About an hour ago, I was just unpacking. Do you need any help with dinner?"

"Don't you dare! That's my job, dearie," Mrs. Morris teased, joining them for a hug.

Mrs. Morris handed Margo a stack of plates and pointed to the adjacent room. Margo hadn't realized the ranch had an extra extension on the back of the building until then.

"You can help Chase set the table. The rest of the ranch staff will be here shortly," Mrs. Morris smiled, heading back to the stove.

"Great," Margo smiled, hoping her father and Mrs. Morris couldn't sense her sarcasm.

When Margo entered the new dining room, she was stunned. It was beautifully decorated – no doubt thanks to Mrs. Morris' input. The dining table looked big enough to sit at least twenty people. Chase was in there already, laying out plates and cutlery over a fresh white tablecloth.

"How many staff does Dad have?" she asked, instantly grabbing Chase's attention.

"Fifteen, including myself and Mrs. Morris. The ranch has grown a lot since you were last here."

"How can he afford that? The last time I was here, this place was falling apart, and Dad could barely make ends meet," Margo frowned.

"A lot has changed. Change is the only constant in life, right?" Using her words against her, Chase winked, something Margo didn't like.

"So, what's your official job title now? Still a ranch hand?"

"Nope, haven't been a ranch hand in almost eight years. I'm ranch manager now," Chase offered, taking the plates from her hands. Of course, she knew that. She was just trying to rile him up. She could see his jaw working, though he kept a friendly smile on his face. Or was it smugness? Either way, she shot herself in the foot because he looked entirely too handsome and too comfortable setting the table in *her* house.

"And the best ranch manager around. I've had several other ranches trying to poach him," her father offered, entering the room with a large pot to put in the middle of the table.

At dinner, Margo sat next to her father and Mrs. Morris. She spent most of the dinner getting acquainted with the rest of the staff and found them to be a wonderful group. They all seemed so happy. From the stories they told, Chase was the best boss they'd ever had. Even though he was challenging at times, they respected him. The ranch went from strength to strength and was more profitable than ever because of him. Her father was even thinking of expanding the ranch, with Chase already in talks with authorities about buying more land.

"Dad, this is incredible," Margo said, grabbing his hand and squeezing it.

"It is all thanks to Chase. I couldn't have done it without him. And one day, all this will be yours."

"Dad, please not this again," Margo complained.

"Like it or not, this is your legacy," her father insisted.

Margo tried to steer the conversation onto other things and grew uncomfortable under Chase's watchful gaze.

CHAPTER 4

Margo lay in bed that night with her father's words circling her mind. All through dinner, he had insisted that whether she liked it or not, the ranch was hers, and it was about time she came to grips with it. She knew her dad didn't want to let the ranch go, especially out of love for her and his memories of her mother. Even with Chase's help, she knew the ranch was taking its toll on her father, and she didn't appreciate him trying to force it on her. She had once loved the ranch, but that love died with her mother. As a result, the ranch held many painful memories.

Unable to sleep, she paced her room, trying to figure out how to navigate the situation. Taking a picture of her mother from the bedside table, Margo looked at it with tears in her eyes. Her mother's face smiled back at her from atop Stormy, her prize-winning mare. Minnie had loved riding and had instilled that love and appreciation for horses into Margo. Margo missed riding, even if she tried to hide it from herself.

Frustrated that she couldn't sleep, she wrapped herself up and headed outside, hoping the cold night air might clear her head. But, of course, she wasn't the only person to have that idea. Heading to the back porch, she bumped into Chase, who sat cross-legged in a chair with a beer bottle in hand.

"Sorry, I didn't realize anyone else was out here," she said.

Chase said nothing and simply pulled his hat further down his face. He was biting his tongue, not wanting to erupt and tell Margo what he thought of her.

"Is it okay if I join you? I did always love this view of the mountains," Margo asked.

"You don't need my permission. This is your property; after all, I'm just an employee," Chase muttered.

"It's not my ranch. It's my father's. I have my life in L.A."

Chase coughed and shook his head before swinging off the rest of his drink, preparing to leave. He stopped several times, turning back, wanting to say what was on his mind.

"Have something to say?" Margo finally challenged.

"Yes, in fact, I do!" Chase snapped. "Your father has put everything into the ranch for *you*, not himself. He isn't the same man he was after your mother died, but he pushed on. All he cares about is that when he is gone, you have something that will provide for you and be a constant reminder of both him and Minnie. Yet all you care about is yourself. You do not know how lucky you are."

Chase didn't stick around for a response. His feelings were made clear. The sad thing was that no matter how angry Margo was at his words, she couldn't argue with them. She had been so blinded by her pain that she had neglected to think of her father and, to some extent, Chase. When they were kids, he'd all but lived in their barn. She hadn't thought much about it then. But she'd found out later things weren't all that great at home for Chase. Chase and her dad had bonded a long time ago.

————

The weather turned quickly, and snow rolled in. Luckily, Margo had come prepared. With Chase's words reminding her of how she had let her father down, she decided to take the time to get to know the inner workings of the ranch. She spent the first few days of her trip with her father, getting to grips with all the administration before reluctantly asking Chase to show her the day-to-day running of the ranch.

Margo wasn't sure if the snow reminded her of past holidays with her family or if it was the passion Chase had for the ranch that brought her around, but she soon found she enjoyed working on the ranch. She didn't realize how much she missed it.

"Don't break his heart," Chase said one day as they saddled up the horses to go for a ride.

"Excuse me?"

"Robert. Don't pretend to enjoy all this only to run off again."

"How dare you!" Margo snapped as she climbed on top of her chosen stallion.

"From what I hear, you are a graphic designer and a damn good one. You can do that from here. You wouldn't be giving up your precious life. Robert needs you. He just won't admit it."

Margo could feel the tears building in her eyes and didn't want to give Chase the satisfaction of seeing her cry.

"You are right; this will be my ranch one day, which means I will be your boss. You will do well watching your tongue around me. How dare you speak to me that way," she snapped.

"Never had someone put you in your place before?" Chase asked.

"Get lost, Chase," Margo snapped, spurring her horse to ride off without him as tears finally started to fall.

After their clash, Margo and Chase only interacted to discuss matters regarding ranch business. She kept her distance and refused to talk to him at dinner. Margo didn't know what annoyed her more, the way he chose to put his point across or that some – not all – of what he said was true.

———

Christmas Eve approached, which meant that her father was hosting a lavish dinner – prepared by Mrs. Morris. To get herself in the mood and to avoid talking to Chase, Margo broke out her box of decorations and sprinkled her love for the holidays all over the ranch. When her father saw the lengths she had gone to, he smiled at her with tears.

"I haven't seen the ranch like this in years. It's good to see that her love for the holidays lives on within you," he kissed his daughter's forehead and drifted to his office, not wanting Margo to see him upset in bittersweet remembrance of his late wife.

Margo climbed the shaky ladder to try and hang her mother's glass snowflake on top of the tree. She had forgotten about the wobbly floorboard by the fireplace, so when the ladder shook, and she almost fell, she dropped the snowflake. It smashed on the floor, leaving Margo heartbroken. She climbed down the ladder and picked up the pieces; unable to stop her tears, she began crying.

"What happened? I heard a crash," Chase asked, panicking as he ran into the room.

"I dropped it. It was hers, and now it...." Margo sobbed.

Chase picked her up and took the broken pieces from her hands.

"Careful; you don't want to cut yourself. I can fix this. Dinner will be served soon. Go freshen up."

Margo didn't argue. She left the broken remains of the snowflake with Chase and ran to her room.

CHAPTER 5

Christmas Eve arrived, and the table was set. Mrs. Morris helped Margo decorate the table with holly and handwritten place cards. Every napkin was embroidered in the corners with a different representation of Christmas. Tinsel hung around the clock, and the back of each hair was covered to look like Santa's hat. It was beautiful.

Everyone was dressed in their Christmas best. The women wore cocktail dresses, the men wore suits, and her father had even broken out a tie – something he never did. Chase wore a simple black suit with a grey shirt and the collar left open. Margo had opted for a red skater dress with green and white trim.

"Can I switch places with you, Mrs. Morris?" Chase asked, much to Margo's surprise.

Margo smiled as Chase took the seat next to her but moved her chair closer to her father. Chase sat silently for a moment before placing a large box wrapped in white paper decorated with gold snowflakes and a red ribbon.

"Merry Christmas," he said.

"Why would you get me something? I didn't get you a gift," Margo whispered as she pulled off the ribbon.

"It's okay. This didn't cost anything but time," Chase answered.

Margo's eyes filled with tears, and a lump climbed up her throat. Inside lay her mother's snowflake. She thought it was in no condition to be repaired, but Chase had somehow managed to fix it.

"Be careful. It still needs a little more time to set."

"I can't tell you what this means to me. Thank you," Margo choked, wrapping her arms around Chase's neck, kissing his cheek gently.

The rest of the meal was pleasant. Everyone exchanged gifts and stories, and to Margo's surprise, she found herself warming to Chase. She thought back over his words, and while he hadn't said them in the nicest way, the sentiment behind them held meaning. He cared, not about himself, but about her father, the ranch, and the other people who called it home. He was selfless from what she had heard, and she couldn't deny that the work he did was amazing. The ranch wouldn't be the same without him.

Margo wondered what had happened to Chase to make him so hard and closed off. Why did he let his temper rule him, and why does he think he is better than everyone else? It didn't show often, but in the short time they had spent together, she had seen glimpses of his softer side and the heart of gold beating in his chest. She also couldn't deny how handsome he was or how she caught him looking at her as the night went on.

"So, what are everyone's plans for New Year's?" Mrs. Morris asked.

"I guess I could extend my trip so I can stay here for the New Year," Margo smiled.

"Extend your trip? You're leaving?" Chase asked; his annoyance was clear for all to see.

"Yes. I was never moving back. I was here for the holidays," Margo answered.

"So why waste my time trying to learn about the ranch?"

"Because this ranch will be mine at some point, I needed to know how it's run."

"Oh, I get it! So, you will just run away again, and what then? Never see your father again? Wait for him to die and just take what's yours?" Chase yelled, standing abruptly. He had a knack for saying the most candid of things.

"I never said that at all, and what business is it of yours?" Margo snapped back.

"I think someone has a crush on Margo and doesn't want her to leave," joked Mrs. Morris.

"Shut up, Sam," Chase barked.

"Don't talk to her like that!" Margo snapped, standing up and glaring Chase down.

"I thought you were better than this, Margo. Your mother would be so…" Chase was cut off when Margo slapped him hard across the face, silencing the room.

"Don't you dare talk about my mother, and don't you dare assume anything about me."

They continued to argue as everyone sat back, gasping, unsure of what to do but unable to look away from the chaos. Chase argued that Margo was self-centered and a money-grabber who didn't care about family. Margo argued that Chase was no different, only caring about his job.

"Of course, I care about the ranch. I might not have had an interest when I started, but something you said to me rang true. I want to continue what my father started, but it was never the plan for me to stay. Why do you care so much?" Margo finally snapped.

Chase fell silent, opening his mouth several times to speak but stopping himself. He knew what he wanted to say but couldn't bring himself to.

"Enough!" roared Robert slamming his hands down on the table.

Everyone turned to look at him, waiting for what he had to say. His face was red with rage, and Margo saw a wave of anger on his face she had never seen before.

"This ranch is not worth it!" Robert roared.

"Robert, don't say that. Look at all we have built; look at what it represents," Chase said.

"Dad…."

"Enough! Margo, do you care about this ranch? Do you want to take over when I'm gone?"

Margo nodded.

"Chase, do you care about this ranch? The people and everything else?"

"This ranch is my life, sir, " Chase answered.

"I want you both to live the lives you want. I want you to have what I had here with Minnie. But I will not stand for all this arguing. You are taking away everything special about it."

He paused, choosing his words carefully, turning his thoughts over in his mind.

"I've come to a decision," Robert said.

What he said next caused everyone in the room to gasp in shock.

"Christmas Day! Margo and Chase will marry...."

"What?" Chase and Margo yelled at once.

"You both claim to care about me and this ranch so much. I say you marry and run it together for a year. If you refuse, I'm selling this ranch and donating the money to a cancer research charity. Take it or leave it," Robert spat out. He rose, dropped his napkin on the table, and stormed out of the room.

CHAPTER 6

Margo and Chase stood dumbfounded, staring at one another. Chase ran off after Robert first, needing answers. Robert's demand was utterly over the top and impulsive. Chase knew Robert didn't make decisions lightly, which begged the question, *how long had Robert been planning this*?

"What happened to ladies first?" Margo snapped, following Chase through the house.

Chase refused to answer. His temper was flaring, and he didn't want to take it out on Margo. His issue wasn't with her; it was with her father.

Robert was exactly where Chase knew he would be – in his office, sitting behind his desk with a glass of whiskey. Robert sat with a red face and a look of thunder. Chase had never seen Robert so angry; he was usually so calm.

"Do you care to explain, Robert?" Chase asked as calmly as he could.

"I think I made my feelings clear," Robert answered.

"Dad, you can't be serious!" Margo snapped as she stormed into the room.

Robert calmly opened his top desk drawer, pulled out a small brown folder, and tossed it across his desk. Margo reached for it, but Chase got there first. He scanned the document with wide eyes before shoving the paper toward Margo.

"How long have you been planning this?" Chase snarled, his anger getting increasingly hard to control.

"You drew up a contract?" Margo gasped.

"Yes, I did. Before you came here, Margo, I had been thinking of signing the ranch over to Chase."

"What?" Margo roared, slamming the contract back on the desk.

"Do not interrupt me again. I've had enough of both of you. I'm tired of no one listening to me. This is the only thing I could think of that would force both of you to listen!" Robert roared.

"Bit extreme, don't you think, Robert?" Chase challenged.

"Be quiet, both of you!" Robert slammed his hand on the desk and waited for them to listen.

"Margo has never shown any interest in the ranch. So, I invited her to give her one last chance to love it like I do."

"I am right here, Dad! Why are you talking about me like I'm not in the room?"

Robert ignored Margo and continued, "Before Margo agreed to spend the holidays here, I was planning on signing the ranch over to you, Chase. You have built this place up in a way I never could, but it wouldn't be fair for me to sign away Margo's inheritance without giving her a chance."

Chase nodded but still needed more answers. The entire scheme was insane.

"Margo, if you had turned to me this trip and said you didn't want the ranch, it would have gone to Chase. However, seeing the love you two *both* have for this place has me conflicted. The ranch is rightfully yours, but Chase has sunk his life, his heart, and soul into this place."

"Of course, I love this place, Dad. It's *home*. I was raised here, but I still don't see how you came up with this plan," Margo said, pulling up a chair in front of the desk.

"You two both have let your life be ruled by work. If that's how you choose to live your life, that's fine. But I want you to at least experience having, with someone, what I had with Minnie. It really is the key to making this place work."

"Yes, but Robert. You and Minnie loved each other. Margo and I...."

"Had a fling ten years ago," Robert interrupted.

Margo and Chase looked at each other in shock. They thought they had hidden their fling well. They thought no one else knew.

"Clearly, there is something there, and you both obviously have trouble deciding what you want, be it a relationship or the ranch. Now you have common ground. I devised this plan, hoping I wouldn't have to enforce it. You get married tomorrow, you live here at the ranch for a year, and if you decide you do not want to stay together, that's fine." Robert relaxed back, folding his arms across his chest.

"I still don't get it," Margo said.

"In that year, it will give you an insight into what is important in life and what both your lives are lacking or not. After that, you will decide between you what happens with the ranch. Margo, if you decide you want the ranch after I'm gone, it's yours. If you decide you don't, it goes to Chase. Or you could decide to split it. Either way, I'm leaving the decision up to you. If you can't meet the contract's terms and stay married while running the ranch for a year, it gets sold. And the money is donated to charity."

Robert's eyes danced between Margo and Chase, waiting for either of them to respond, but they were both in such a state of shock that they didn't speak. It was a lot of information, and they didn't have much time to think it through.

"I shall leave you two to make up your mind. But be quick about it; we may have a wedding to plan," Robert said, leaving the room.

CHAPTER 7

Margo sat on the back porch wrapped in a blanket guarding against the winter's chill, a cup of cocoa in hand. She heard Chase approach and sit in the seat next to her, but she said nothing. She had run over what her father had said so many times but still had no answer that she liked.

"I say we do it," Chase finally spoke, popping the top of his beer bottle.

"You can't be serious?" Margo laughed.

"Deadly," Chase answered.

"We can't stand each other. This is a crazy plan; he can't force us to marry," Margo snipped.

"Oh yes, he can. I've read that contract five times; it's airtight. We have to be married, but nowhere in that contract does it say that we have to share a bed. So, when the year is up, we get the marriage annulled and be done with it."

"What makes you think I will agree to this?" Margo asked, finally turning to face Chase.

"You don't want some stranger running this ranch any more than I do. I'm not saying it's a great plan, but it's just a year."

"Why are you so calm about this?" Margo inquired.

"Oh, believe me, I am anything but calm, but I don't see any other choice."

"Chase, I'm not marrying you."

"It's not a real marriage Margo!" Chase snapped, jumping to his feet and pacing the deck. "Look, can I be straight with you?"

Margo nodded, sitting up straighter and listening. She could tell he was having difficulty opening up to someone he couldn't stand.

"If your dad sells this place tomorrow, sure, it will hurt you for a bit. All your memories with your mother are here, but eventually, you will get over it. You have a life in L.A., you have a career. I….this ranch is my life. These people are my life. We need to think of the other people who call this place their home too. It's not just about us," Chase rubbed the back of his neck nervously.

"Chase?" Margo walked over and forced him to look her in the eye. "Be honest with me."

Chase sighed heavily, then looked into Margo's emerald green eyes, the eyes she had gotten from her mother.

"Without this ranch, I have nothing."

"Dad told me other ranches had headhunted you; you would find another job."

"It wouldn't be the same."

"Why?"

Chase's jaw tensed; he was holding back his answer. Margo waited, but Chase stood still, unwilling to answer.

"How do you think we can make this work?" Margo asked.

"We marry, we split the duties of the ranch, I will take most of the heavy lifting so you can still concentrate on your graphic design, and we live in separate bedrooms. After a year, we dissolve the marriage and split the ranch 50/50," Chase offered.

"Who's to say, in that time, I decide I love this place and don't want to split it?"

"Then I guess I'm trusting that you won't screw me over and leave me at the end of this with nothing. Because let's face it, Kitten, if you don't marry me tomorrow, you can kiss your inheritance bye-bye," Chase growled, his temper coming through in his words and eyes.

"Wow, and even to protect my inheritance, why would I risk marrying someone who clearly has a temper?"

"You are not perfect yourself, Kitten."

"Stop calling me that!" Margo snapped.

Chase chuckled, Margo had proved his point, and she knew it.

"Do we have a deal?" Chase offered out his hand.

Margo looked at it, then back up at Chase. She wasn't considering this was she? If only she could convince her father to give them a little more time to figure things out, to offer another solution. But she knew Robert was a stubborn man, and even if she devised a better plan, her father would dig in his heels. It was where she got her stubborn streak from.

"There has to be another way," she whispered, suddenly overwhelmed with the implications of what she was about to do.

Chase stepped forward and cupped her face with his hand, wiping away a stray tear with his thumb.

"I know this isn't easy, but we both know Robert. He is as stubborn as the ranch mule. Nothing is going to change his mind. I will not force you to do this if you do not want to," Chase offered.

"I don't know what to do," Margo sobbed.

She had always dreamed of her wedding day – A fairytale wedding with her mother's wedding dress, the man of her dreams, and her father walking her down the aisle. This was not the wedding day she planned or wanted. She thought about the other people who called the ranch home, Mikey, Rachel, Harvey, Mrs. Morris, and many more. She thought about the memories of her mother and father's laughter over the years. Then she thought of Chase and everything he had done for her father, how he had brought him back from the brink and never left his side when other offers were presented. There was so much more at stake than herself. She had to agree.

"Go and tell my father he gets his wish. I can't look at him right now," Margo breathed, pushing herself away from Chase and running to her room.

She didn't want Chase to see her cry.

CHAPTER 8

Margo had hardly slept; her eyes were puffy and red from crying. Mrs. Morris knocked lightly on her bedroom before letting herself in and opening the curtains letting the winter sun flood the room.

"Morning, sweetie," Mrs. Morris' voice was somber; she didn't like the situation any more than Margo and Chase did.

"Morning, Mrs. Morris," Margo yawned, rubbing her face, trying to hide her tear-stained cheeks.

"Margo, come on, call me Sam," Sam sat on the end of Margo's bed, her face filled with regret.

"What is it, Samantha?"

"The wedding is planned for three o'clock, in the barn. He has set aside your mother's dress for you too."

That was the final straw. Margo stormed out of bed and down the hall to her father's room. He wasn't there, so she headed to his office. Chase was heading inside from the morning chores when Margo flew down the stairs in her pink and white spotted P.J. shorts and camisole that hugged her curves and showed off her long legs. Her thick black hair was still messy from tossing and turning all night long, but it framed her face beautifully.

"Margo?" Chase asked.

She glanced at him before storming into her father's office. She pushed the door so hard that it slammed against the wall.

"You may be forcing me into this marriage, but don't you dare for a second think that I will be wearing Mom's dress or getting married in the barn. She would be ashamed of you! If I am doing this, it's on my terms, and we will get married at city hall!" Margo roared.

"Margo...." Robert began, but Margo was too angry to listen.

"Those are my terms! Deal with it!" she snapped back before storming out and back upstairs.

Chase watched her storm off, he had never seen her so angry, but he knew it was more than that. She was hurting, and it pained him to see. It wasn't just Robert forcing her into this. Chase felt guilty for putting his concerns on her the night before. If he hadn't mentioned everyone else relying on the ranch, she might have decided against the marriage altogether. Shame flooded him as he followed her upstairs.

"Margo? Are you okay?" Chase asked, knocking gently on her door.

Margo paced angrily around the room. When she turned to look at him, he saw the pain in her eyes. He didn't want to be a reason for that pain.

"Am I *okay*? Nothing about this is okay! He thinks he is giving me something when he is taking something far more precious...." Margo stopped abruptly.

"Look, ignore what I said last night. The others and I will deal with whatever happens. If you don't want to do this, you don't have to."

"How can I ignore it when everything you said is true? It's not just you or me we have to consider here."

"Margo."

"No, Chase! It's done! I've made the call. The wedding is set for four-thirty this afternoon at city hall. I don't want to see anyone until then," she slammed the door in his face.

———

Margo spent the rest of the day walking around the ranch, purposefully avoiding everyone she may bump into. She couldn't stand the looks of pity or judgment. She didn't have to hear the whispers to know the word around the ranch, the stories on the wind judging her and Chase for going through with Robert's insane demand.

She walked for as long as she could before she knew she had to prepare for her wedding. A sham marriage she was being forced into by the man who was supposed to love and protect her. She took a long hot shower before putting on a simple but flattering green velvet cocktail dress. If she were doing this, she wouldn't wear a wedding dress, especially not her mother's.

She drove to city hall alone. Pulling up outside, she saw her father and Mrs. Morris waiting. She checked her makeup in the mirror and told herself to be strong before striding toward the door. Robert outstretched his arms for a hug, but Margo glared back at him and walked inside.

"It might not be a real wedding, but every bride deserves a beautiful bouquet," smiled Samantha handing Margo a small, simple bouquet of her favorite flowers from the ranch. Margo smiled and offered Samantha a quick hug in thanks. Robert straightened his tie and offered Margo his arm.

"You can't be serious?" Margo snipped.

"Excuse me?" Robert gasped.

"You do not get the honor of walking me down the aisle when you are forcing me into this."

Margo turned away and waited for her father and Samantha to walk inside in front of her. The advantage of a small town was that asking the Mayor to open city hall for a quick wedding ceremony on Christmas Day was no big deal, since he was planning on attending it at the ranch anyway. Then, taking one more breath, she walked in with her head held high. Chase was waiting in a simple black suit with a black shirt and green tie. His jaw dropped open when he saw her. His eyes were glued to her as she walked toward him.

"I guess your father was right. We are a match," Chase whispered, tugging on his tie and pointing at her dress.

He knew his comment wasn't wanted from the angry look Margo gave him.

"Sorry, just trying to make light of the situation. All jokes aside, you look beautiful," Chase smiled.

"I guess you don't look too bad yourself," she responded, trying her hardest to suppress a smile.

The ceremony began, but Margo didn't hear a thing. Her mind glossed over, but she pasted a smile on her face. She repeated the vows required and placed a white gold band on Chase's finger. Margo slipped into a safe space in her mind, protecting herself from snapping and breaking down in tears.

Chase, taking her hand, snapped her back to reality. His hand was rough against her skin from years of manual work, but his touch was soft and gentle. It caught Margo off guard, and she looked up at him and was captivated by his eyes. He slid the ring on her finger and held her hand tighter.

"Can I say something?" Chase asked; the officiant nodded their response.

"I need you to hear me when I say this, Margo. We may not have gotten here easily. But I am a man of my word. I take these vows seriously. So believe me when I say, as long as we are married, as long as you are my wife, I have your back. I will help and support you in any way I can and aim to make you as happy as possible. I will be a friend, a confident, and the best husband I can be."

Margo didn't know how but she knew he meant every word and that as long as they were legally married, she would be safe with him. She gasped her surprise and smiled softly. She thought she knew Chase, but she had never seen his soft, sincere side before. She liked it.

"It gives me great pleasure to announce you, man and wife. You may kiss the bride."

They hadn't discussed this part of the wedding, and Margo froze when Chase placed a hand on her hip and gently pulled her to him. A touch that sent electricity running through her entire body. Her breath caught in her throat when he placed a hand around the back of her neck, playing with her hair as he brought his lips down to hers.

CHAPTER 9

Chase hadn't meant to kiss Margo at the altar. But in the moment, it seemed like the right thing to do. Only a select few at the wedding knew the truth. They had to play the part for everyone else. So why hadn't he been able to get that kiss off his mind? Why was he lying in bed sleepless, thinking about how soft her lips felt and how much he wanted to do it again?

It's been a while, that's all. There is nothing more to it, Chase tried to convince himself.

After the ceremony, Margo hadn't stuck around. She had ignored her father and jumped right in her car to head home. Chase had been left there explaining to the other guests that it was only a simple wedding. They hadn't planned on having a reception or any fuss. Soon after, he headed back himself. He ventured to her room to see if she was okay, but it was empty. Chase searched high and low but couldn't find her. Mrs. Morris had put out Christmas dinner, but it sat untouched and alone.

I guess no one else is in the mood for a feast either, Chase thought.

Hooves pounded in the backyard, and soon after, the horse whinnied as its rider jumped down. Heading to the back, Chase saw Margo leading Harvey, the ranch's biggest, baddest stallion, back to the stables. Her face was flushed from riding in the cold. Her pale skin was highlighted with pink hues. She locked eyes with Chase, and he saw something he had never seen before – A cold hardness that said she was blocking out the world.

"Harvey is known for being an angry horse. He is picky about who he lets ride him. In protest, he has kicked out at some of the ranch's most experienced ranch hands, people he has been around his entire life. I'm impressed he let you ride him," Chase said, leaning against the barn door as he watched Margo de-saddle.

"Well, I guess he could sense my anger," Margo mumbled.

"Want to talk about it?"

Margo shot Chase a death stare that told him to shut up and leave her alone. Chase held up his hands in surrender and turned to leave.

"I don't know if you are interested, but Christmas dinner is on the table. I don't think anyone else is eating, and it's a shame for it to go to waste," Chase shot back over his shoulder.

Margo mumbled something he didn't quite hear, but he pressed on anyway.

"I know Christmas is your favorite time of year. This day might not have been the Christmas at home you planned, but it doesn't mean we can't still keep some of the magic alive."

———

Chase leaned over the table and began lighting candles. He opened a bottle of red wine and poured two glasses. Checking the food, it was still warm, but it wouldn't be for much longer. Slicing some turkey, he began to prepare a plate for himself when Margo silently joined him.

"Normally, I would be ecstatic for Christmas dinner. Now, it's tainted," she whispered.

"Then let's eat and drink the memory away," Chase said, handing her a glass of wine.

They sat and ate in silence for a full two courses. The food was delicious. Mrs. Morris had outdone herself. Margo was famished; she hadn't eaten all day, too busy feeling nauseous about the decision they had just made. When they were both ready for dessert, two bottles of wine sat empty in the center of the table.

Silence lay thick in the air. It wasn't uncomfortable to their surprise. They were pretty content sitting with each other, enjoying a delicious meal without a word being spoken. But silence could only offer comfort for so long. They were in this together now, and there was much to discuss.

"Feeling better?" Chase asked as he finished his Christmas pudding.

"I don't want to talk about it."

"I gathered that when you left me at the altar, Mrs. Adams."

"Who said I was taking your name?" Margo grinned.

"Whatever you're feeling, it's best to discuss it now so we can move on and get through the rest of the year as best we can."

"So sensitive," Margo snapped, pouring another glass of wine.

"If you don't want to talk about what's on your mind, then let's discuss splitting the duties of the ranch. What's your work schedule like? What tasks would you prefer? I'm more than happy to do all the heavy lifting; you can stick with the admin. I wouldn't want you to break a nail."

Margo slammed her hand on the table and leaped to her feet, "This is just great. Merry Christmas, Margo!"

"Excuse me?"

"My father is supposed to care for me. He is supposed to know me. Yet he not only takes my favorite time of year and taints it with his demand but also takes away my wedding day. He has ruined my mother's memory and made it seem like he is doing it to help me."

"Margo, it's just a day."

"No, Chase, it's not. Every girl dreams of her wedding day. When Mom died, I dreamt of keeping her there with me on my special day by wearing her dress. Instead, Dad demanded that to keep the home where I can still see her in every nook and cranny, I had to enter into a sham marriage. But you know what the kicker is? He chose to betray me on my favorite day of the year. The day that was special to her," Margo yelled, finally letting out her frustration.

"You didn't wear her dress."

"He wanted me to. But you know what? It doesn't matter. You said it yourself. It's just a day. So how are we going to get through this year?"

CHAPTER 10

The rest of the evening didn't go much better. They argued back and forth about splitting the duties. Margo didn't like how Chase mansplained everything as if she were a child. Chase didn't think Margo was capable of the heavier duties and forbid her from touching any of the machinery.

"You forbid me? You are my husband on paper and paper alone. You can't forbid me from doing anything!" Margo snapped.

"You have no mechanical experience. Not only could you hurt yourself, but you could damage the machines, and those things are expensive enough to repair, let alone replace. End of discussion. You are to stay away from the milking machines, the tractors, and everything else that has an engine!" Chase roared back.

Margo wanted to argue further, but she knew he was right. Still, she didn't like him telling her what to do.

"So now all the duties have been split, let's get down to the awkward part." Margo asserted.

"Awkward?"

"How do we navigate this marriage for the rest of the year?" Margo asked.

"I thought we had already discussed that. We assess the running of the ranch, decide what we both want and then split or sell at the end of the year. We do not share a bed so that we can get a clean-cut annulment at the end of it."

Margo nodded, but Chase could sense there was more to her asking. He saw the same hurt and pain in her eyes when she spoke about how her father had tainted her mother's memory.

"Margo, I need you to listen very closely to what I am about to say because I will only say it once. I made a vow to you today...."

"As long as we are married, as long as you are my wife, I have your back. I will help and support you in any way I can and aim to make you as happy as possible. I will be a friend, a confident, and the best husband I can be," Margo repeated, shocking Chase that she had remembered.

"I meant it. Let's just get through this year as pain-free as possible."

———

New Year's Eve approached quicker than either of them expected. With the help of Samantha and, reluctantly, Robert, Margo planned a celebration with the hopes of putting all the sourness of Christmas behind them. However, Chase wasn't too happy when he found out Margo had invited his parents.

"*Why* did you invite them?"

"I want to meet my in-laws," Margo answered simply.

"This isn't a real marriage, Margo! Uninvite them! Now!" Chase demanded.

Chase avoided Margo for the rest of the day. And when the party started, she was concerned when she couldn't find him anywhere. Then, finally, his parents arrived, and Margo quickly picked up why Chase didn't want them around. While his mother was sweet enough, Margo would have to be blind to miss her disapproving and side-eye looks. His father was worse. While Margo talked about all the great work that Chase had done, all his father could concentrate on was the fact he had turned down several opportunities for more money. They were tiring people, and the more time Margo spent with them, the more she decided she didn't like their company.

Just after the midnight celebration, Margo detached from the party and wandered to her favorite spot on the back porch. When she arrived, she saw a shadow heading to the barn. Curiosity made her follow, and she was right. Sitting with Harvey, surrounded by a few empty beer bottles, sat Chase.

"Happy New Year," Margo smiled.

Chase raised his bottle and drank to toast, but his face was somber.

"I'm sorry I invited your parents. I thought…."

"You didn't think, but it doesn't matter. They will be gone soon."

"I see now why you didn't want them here."

"I don't want to talk about it," Chase snapped.

Margo nodded and joined him on the hay bales, scooping up a bottle and drinking in silence. She had hoped that he might open up the way she had, but Chase wasn't just a closed door. He was a door guarded with an iron padlock.

"I'm off to bed," Margo finally spoke, deciding it was better to give up.

"Margo," Chase stood, grabbing her wrist gently, stopping her from leaving.

"Happy New Year," Chase pulled her in and planted a soft, gentle kiss on her lips.

CHAPTER 11

Reminiscent of their wedding day, after New Year's, Margo and Chase pretended the kiss hadn't happened. Of course, they didn't discuss it. But that didn't stop their minds from wandering. Each time Chase kissed Margo, he felt something deep inside that he wanted to explore. Was it that he liked her? Or was it simply the simmering feelings from years ago that he hadn't completely forgotten. It didn't matter because Margo never brought it up.

At first, things seemed to be going according to plan. Margo took three days a week to work on her graphic design and spent four days working with Chase. Then, soon after the wedding, her father moved out of the ranch to a small cottage on the outskirts of town. Margo was happy to see him leave because she was still angry at him. But when Mrs. Morris explained he had moved out so that Chase and Margo could enjoy married life without him under foot, it enraged Margo even more.

With Mrs. Morris' help, Margo quickly got to grips with the administrative side of ranching and decided the best course of action was to avoid Chase altogether. So, she spent the rest of her time working with the other ranch staff.

But the honeymoon stage didn't last long.

Chase stormed across the paddock to where Margo was helping one of the new ranch hands fix a fence the bulls had trashed.

"What the hell is this?" Chase roared, waving a piece of paper in the air.

"I don't know, but I'm sure you are about to tell me," Margo took off her gloves and folded her arms, waiting for Chase to explode.

"You are selling half the cows, two of the mares, and are studding out Harvey?"

"Yes, I am. The cows I'm selling haven't been producing for the ranch for a while, so they are eating funds that could be better suited elsewhere. The money from the mares' sale will go toward buying another stallion for us to breed while Harvey is out on loan."

"You have been here for all of *five minutes*! You have no idea what money those mares bring in or what is going on with those cows. And don't even get me started on Harvey," Chase roared.

"The figures speak for themselves. I've seen the numbers."

"Numbers mean jack. If you took the time to speak to me, you would realize that they have brought in money in other ways. You sell them, and this place will start losing money. I have been running this ranch for almost a decade!"

"And now we are running it together! This is my ranch, Chase."

"Our ranch! We are married, remember Kitten? And I didn't sign any prenup," Chase snapped before storming off, leaving Margo to stew in her thoughts.

———

Things went from bad to worse over the following weeks. They argued over everything and anything, never discussing anything calmly, so everything escalated out of proportion. Margo's animosity toward Chase grew with every passing day. It drove her crazy that, every time they argued, he would remind her they were married and in this together.

Tensions grew. Their arguing started affecting everyone and everything on the ranch. The other workers were reluctant to start tasks

Margo gave them without first checking with Chase, and suppliers were not willing to renegotiate deals with Chase without Margo's approval. It wasn't long before the ranch began to suffer, losing money at an alarming rate. And maintenance was not getting done.

"You refused to pay the repairs of the milking machine?" Chase snapped as he stormed into Margo's – formally Robert's – office.

"I didn't refuse," Margo sighed, rubbing her hands over her face in frustration.

"Then what did you do? Because without that machine, we start losing money!"

"We *are* losing money already, Chase! Why do you think we can't pay for the repairs?" Margo tossed a file across the table.

Chase snatched up the documents and scanned them. He looked up in alarm and slammed them back down.

"Crap! The ranch hasn't performed this bad in years," Chase sighed.

Sitting in the chair in front of her desk, Chase hunched over and rested his face in his hands. Margo poured them each a glass of whiskey and placed a drink in front of Chase.

"What are we doing here, Chase?"

"What do you mean?"

"If we carry on like this, the ranch will fail. We clearly can't work together. If the ranch fails, we have gone through with this sham of a marriage for nothing."

"What are you saying?"

"Come on. You can't tell me you haven't felt like giving up too?"

Chase's jaw tensed before he finished his glass in one gulp, wincing from the burn.

"The thought had crossed my mind," he admitted, pouring himself a second glass.

"So, what do we do?"

Giving up would be the easier option. If they continued at the rate they were going, the ranch wouldn't see summer. They talked, argued, and talked some more until the early hours of the following morning. Finally, they agreed that they would never see eye to eye. Chase thought Margo was clueless about anything to do with the ranch, and Margo thought him an ill-tempered egotist. Margo argued that she might understand things quicker if he was a better teacher. Chase asserted that she was out of her league.

But they could agree that they both cared for the ranch, its employees, and livestock. It was the only thing they possibly could agree on. So, they had decided that Chase would explain everything in detail, and Margo would no longer block his plans. If they disagreed on something, they would discuss it maturely and get the ranch back to its thriving state.

Slowly and on shaky legs, things began to pick up. The ranch swiftly started to recover. Samantha had even made a few passing comments that it seemed Margo and Chase were getting along and made a good couple – A statement that they both chose to ignore. However, their suppressed grins were still observed by everyone.

———

Spring came around quickly, with Chase and Margo following into a comfortable step. The closer they worked together, the more Chase found he admired Margo. She was a hard worker, a quick learner, and often put others' needs above her own. She had sacrificed her wedding day to save Chase and the others; he hadn't seen it that way before.

Margo couldn't deny that Chase was flawed. He was quick to anger, bossy and pig-headed, but he had a softer side. It didn't come out much, but she clung to the memory for days when she saw it. She was starting to see Chase in a new light, and to her shock, she liked what she saw. He was tender with the animals. And while his method was not to her taste, she could see why everyone admired him so much.

CHAPTER 12

Summer arrived, and with it came Margo's thirtieth birthday. Margo originally planned to go to Vegas with her friends from L.A., Rachel and Michelle. But since working on the ranch, she had canceled. Her graphic design career was also taking a hit. While she loved her job, she enjoyed working on the ranch so much that she missed deadlines, and the work she submitted became subpar.

Rachel and Michelle had harassed Margo for days over the phone; they believed she was putting the ranch above their friendship and her work. Margo liked Rachel and Michelle, but they were more like associates than actual friends, so she wasn't too bothered when their calls stopped coming. Their comments, on the other hand, cut deep.

"Hey, a penny for your thoughts?" Chase asked.

Margo had been sitting at her desk staring into mid-air mindlessly for so long she had lost track of time.

"Huh? Oh, nothing. What's up?"

Chase pulled a small box from around his back and placed it on her desk.

"Happy Birthday," Chase smiled.

"You remembered?"

"What kind of husband would I be if I didn't know my wife's birth-day?" Chase grinned.

Margo offered him a look. Months ago, they had agreed to no longer refer to each other as husband and wife or to throw the marriage into each other's faces. They had boiled their situation down to what it was – a business transaction and nothing more.

Chase took the hint and raised his hands in surrender. They had agreed to stop, but he couldn't help but notice how her cheeks flushed red. And she struggled not to smile whenever he called her his wife.

"You didn't have to get me anything."

"It's nothing much."

Margo opened the box to find the typical guy gift: soaps, scrubs, candles. Margo could tell that Chase wasn't one for buying gifts, and looking at the kind gesture, she realized there was still a lot about each other they didn't know.

"Thank you, Chase," Margo smiled, placing the box into her desk drawer.

"You going to tell me what's on your mind?"

"I'm fine."

"You are a rubbish liar, Margo. It's work, isn't it? The ranch has taken over your life, and your true dream is suffering because of it."

Margo's jaw dropped open. She couldn't understand how he had read her mind. Deciding it was better not to argue, she nodded.

"Let me handle the ranch for a few weeks. Take a step back and concentrate on your graphic design. But first, take the rest of the day off. It's your birthday, after all. So, what do you have planned?" Chase asked.

"Nothing," Margo shrugged.

"What? No spa day? No drinks with the girls? Thirty is a big one; you need to celebrate."

"Just because I moved to L.A., that's how you think I would spend my birthday?" Margo laughed.

"Didn't you have plans to go to Vegas?"

"How did you?.... Samantha."

"Bingo."

"Yes, but it doesn't matter anymore," Margo answered, her voice pained.

"They canceled? Some friends."

———

After her brief chat with Chase, Margo decided to take Harvey for a ride. She had grown close to the horse over the last few months, and everyone had noticed how Margo was the only person the horse seemed to react to positively.

After her ride, she headed for a hot shower. When she went back to her room, she found a black cocktail dress with matching heels, a red blazer, and a red leather clutch bag presented beautifully on her bed. There was a note on top of the dress:

No one should spend their thirtieth alone.

When she turned the note over, she found details for a dinner reservation at The Crystal Champagne Glass. It was an upscale champagne bar two towns over. With a smile and butterflies in her stomach, Margo dressed, did her hair, and put on her makeup.

As she descended the stairs, Margo's breath caught in her throat. Chase stood by the front door in dark jeans, a grey shirt, and a black blazer holding a single white rose. His hair was gelled back, and the beard he had grown over the last few months was gone. He looked amazing.

Her breath quickened, and her pulse began to race, which startled Margo. Was she starting to feel something for Chase? Or was it just his gesture that had her flustered?

"Wow, Margo, you look beautiful," Chase breathed, offering the rose.

"Thank you. You don't look too shabby yourself. It's good to see the beard is gone, too," Margo smiled, running her finger over his jaw.

They locked eyes, and Margo noticed how he visibly tensed.

"Come on, we have a reservation," Chase scooped his hand around Margo's lower back and led her toward his car.

Margo felt her skin light on fire at his touch. She couldn't explain it, but she was starting to feel something she couldn't place.

———

Things got off to an awkward start, primarily due to Margo feeling self-conscious about being the only one drinking. But it was safety first as Chase was driving. The conversation started slowly; all they had discussed since their wedding and her arrival before Christmas. It had been years since their fling, and they had changed significantly. Did they have anything in common? What topics could and couldn't be discussed? Both seemed too nervous to venture into that subject.

"First date nerves, darling? Don't worry. If things don't work out with him, you can always give me a call," winked a somewhat intoxicated guy in a faded blue suit.

Margo glanced over to Chase, whose jaw had tensed, and his eyes darkened. He was clearly, and well within his rights to be, annoyed at the gesture. Margo leaned closer to Chase and took his hand, ensuring their wedding rings were on show.

"Sorry, sugar, I'm quite happily married. Better luck next time. Why don't you head home to your wife? Just because you have removed the ring doesn't mean I can't see the tan lines," Margo winked.

She enjoyed the bemused look on the drunk's face before he staggered off and tried again with the next girl along the bar.

"He is going to try that line with the wrong couple and get a smack in the mouth," Margo laughed.

"If you hadn't stepped in, I was about to," Chase said, sipping his soda.

"Why?" Margo asked, curious and feeling a little more confident now her third champagne had kicked in.

"Be this a sham marriage or not, I don't like guys leering at you like that. What happened to manners and respect? You are a beautiful, intelligent woman. You deserve better than being drooled over by some drunk guy who can barely stand."

Margo was stunned; she hadn't expected an answer like that in her wildest dreams. Moving the hair from her face, she tried to hide her blushing cheeks.

"You are not so bad, Chase," she smiled.

"I may act the jerk sometimes, but I would have to be blind or made of stone not to appreciate what a fine woman you are. That is why I take my vows so seriously. Whatever got us into this, the fact remains, we are married. I know how much marriage means to you, so I don't want the memories of your first marriage to be unpleasant," Chase shrugged.

"I think I may have underestimated you, Chase Adams."

"How so?" he asked.

Margo failed to reply. The butterflies in her stomach had kicked up a million percent. She didn't know if it was the champagne or the compliments Chase was firing her way. He was going to such an effort to make her birthday special. Yet some part of her felt like he was still closed off or didn't truly want to be there. She longed to see him smile, but the thought initially confused her. Why did she want to see him smile?

Slowly, Chase began to open up. The more Margo pushed, the more his walls came down. Eventually, she didn't just get him to smile, she brought him to laugh. It was a deep belly-shaking laugh that caused nearby patrons to look and stare. But Margo loved it.

"You know Chase, I think that is the first time I've heard you laugh."

"You might be right."

As the night drew on, Margo became increasingly intoxicated until, eventually, Chase insisted on going home. Chase tried not to laugh as he struggled to keep Margo standing. Apparently, she wasn't used to heels so high. Add that to the large consumption of alcohol, and the poor girl could barely stay standing. Eventually, he got her safely in the car, and she drifted off to sleep after a few minutes. Chase often glanced over to ensure she was okay and chuckled to himself when she let out a soft drunken snore.

When they arrived back at the ranch, Chase tried to wake her, but she was in a deep sleep. Scooping her into his arms, he carried her up to the door. Struggling to get the keys out of his pocket, he almost let her slip from his arms, catching her just in time. Margo stared ever so slightly, then snuggled closer into his chest. Her hair tickled his nose, and he inhaled softly; she smelled delicious. Before he let his thoughts get the better of him, he forced the door open and carried her to her bed.

Chase stood watching her sleep for longer than he intended. He couldn't seem to pull himself away from how perfect she looked. To his surprise, it was a rather pleasant evening. His aim was purely to be a nice guy, but something had changed. Deciding not to think more about it, he turned to leave.

"Chase?" asked a sleepy voice from behind him.

"Yes."

"Thank you for tonight; I had a wonderful time. You are a nice guy after all," Margo yawned, rolling over onto her stomach and wrapping her arms around her pillow.

"You are really drunk," Chase chuckled softly.

"Not that drunk. Good night, Chase."

"Sweet dreams, Margo."

CHAPTER 13

The following morning, Margo woke to find a cold bottle of water, a glass of freshly squeezed orange juice, and some painkillers on her bedside table. Resting against them sat a note:

Just in case you need it.

Margo smiled. It was obviously from Chase. Her thoughts returned to the night before; she remembered laughing a lot. She remembered how his eyes creased and the melodic tone of his laugh and waking up as he carried her to bed. He was a sweet, kind soul guarded by a tough exterior. She wondered what had made him so cold to the world.

Showering and refreshing her hair and face, she headed downstairs and was pleased to see that Chase was still eating breakfast in the dining room.

"Morning!" Margo smiled, leaning slightly further over the table than needed to reach for the coffee pot.

She tried to hide her smile when Chase's eyes lingered, and he seemed speechless for once.

"How's your head?" Chase asked after clearing his throat and finally averting his gaze.

"Not as bad as I expected. Thanks again for last night. You are pretty fun; who knew?" Margo teased, plucking a slice of toast from the sharing platter in the center of the table.

"I knew. You just never gave me a chance," Chase grinned.

"Well, maybe I will see your fun side again soon," Margo winked.

It wasn't until she noticed him watching her for the fifth time while they ate breakfast that she realized she had been subtly flirting and enjoying it immensely. What it meant, she didn't know. The thought of actually falling for Chase surprised her. But was it such a bad surprise?

Of course, it is! What if he doesn't feel the same way? What if he is playing a game to get half the ranch? He was flirting back, wasn't he? Margo's mind raced.

Weeks passed with many flirtatious looks, subtle touches and the occasional innuendo tossed about. Everyone at the ranch had noticed how the arguing had stopped all of a sudden. And not only were Margo and Chase getting along, but they were also thriving. They had grown so used to each other that they were finishing each other's sentences.

"Do I sense love in the air?" Samantha asked one evening while preparing dinner.

Margo looked out of the kitchen window at Chase chopping wood in the backyard. Her heart picked up pace, and her mouth ran dry.

"I can't say it's love....but I won't rule out infatuation," she admitted.

———

As summer ended and fall began to turn, the leaves in the trees became hues of orange and brown. Chase was oblivious that his life was about to take a drastic left turn. Margo was finishing her latest design project in her office when a rather loud and amorous knock startled her.

She barely had time to save her project and stand up from her desk when a worried Samantha ran into the room.

"Margo, Mrs. Adams is here."

"Who?"

"Your mother-in-law, who else?" chimed Chase's mother as she forced her way into the room.

Margo tried to hide her surprise and smiled sweetly.

"Mrs. Adams, it's so nice to see you. To what do we owe the pleasure?" Margo asked.

"Can't a mother come by and see her son and daughter-in-law?" Mrs. Adams asked, helping herself to a glass of whiskey from the sideboard.

Margo glanced at her watch. It was barely eleven in the morning.

"Shall I go and find Chase?" Samantha asked.

"Of course, what else are you paid for?" Mrs. Adams remarked, waving Mrs. Morris off dismissively.

Margo bit the inside of her cheek hard. She didn't like anyone talking to Mrs. Morris in such a way. But this was Chase's mother, and they had been getting along so well lately she didn't want to mess that up.

Margo talked with Mrs. Adams while they waited for Mrs. Morris to return with Chase. Every comment and snippy remark that fell from Mrs. Adams' lips rubbed Margo the wrong way. She could now see where Chase got his temper from but still couldn't understand how such a vile woman had raised such a kind and caring man.

It became clear to Margo quickly that all Mrs. Adams cared about was status, money, and keeping up with others' opinions. She didn't have a very high opinion of her son. She was constantly comparing him to his older sister, Eleanor, and dismissing all the hard work he had done.

"Mother? What are you doing here?" Chase asked, his face stern, arms folded tightly across his chest.

"Do I need a reason to see my son?"

"You? Yes, now what do you want?" Chase replied.

"I missed you at New Year's, and I have tried to reach out since, but you haven't answered my calls." Mrs. Adams answered, walking over to Chase to wrap him in a hug.

Chase was as stiff as a board and made no effort to return the favor.

It pained Margo to see how much he was struggling. He was uncomfortable in his mother's company.

"There is a reason for that, Mother."

"You pain me, son. Now, why don't you and your wife give me a
tour of this wonderful ranch?"

Margo didn't miss the dismissive emphasis on the words *wife* and
ranch. And from the flash of anger in Chase's eyes, he didn't miss it
either. Margo mouthed, 'I got you,' to Chase as she led Mrs. Adams
around the main house.

Margo played the doting daughter-in-law role well. Ignoring all the
disgruntled looks, the disapproving glances, little groans, and sighs as
they entered room after room. But she wanted to give Mrs. Adams the
benefit of the doubt and showed her the bar, the cows, the milking
room, the stables, and everything else that any normal person would
be impressed with.

After their tour, they settled on the back porch with some drinks.
Chase hadn't said a word since they left the office, keeping himself a
few steps behind and watching his mother closely.

"It's....just a glorified farm, isn't it?"

"I suppose so," Margo chuckled.

"Chase? This is how you have chosen to live your life? Look at what
your sister has made of herself. I feel like I have wasted so much time
on you. It saddens me, truly," Mrs. Adams said.

It horrified Margo how genuinely pained Mrs. Adams sounded as
if Chase's life choices had done her some disservice. How could a
mother talk about her son in such a way? Margo looked over to Chase,
whose head hung low. Margo reached under the table and took hold of
Chase's knee, giving him a gentle, reassuring squeeze.

"I like what I do, Mother. It makes me happy. A concept I'm sure
you and Father would never understand."

"Oh, please. This? Really? Shoveling animal waste makes you
happy? You could have been so much more."

That was the final straw. Margo had heard enough.

"Excuse me, Mrs. Adams, but if it weren't for Chase and all his hard
work, this place would have failed years ago. He has made it the
success it is. He has been headhunted several times from other ranches

because they know what he can do. He is one of the most intelligent men I have ever met," Margo snapped.

"That's my point. He is capable of so much more than this little place. Why turn down the chance for more money? Why stay stagnant? Think of what that brain could do. You could manage a major business and be earning millions," Mrs. Adams argued.

"There are more important things in life than money, Mother."

"Oh please, money makes the world go around. I just want the best for you, son. You could be so much more than a ranch hand," Mrs. Adams sneered.

"Mrs. Adams! I will not have you speaking to my husband like that. I do not care if he is your son; you will give him the respect he deserves. He is the best ranch manager within miles, and you should be as proud of him as I am," Margo yelled, silencing the porch.

Suddenly, Mrs. Adams burst into laughter, "Oh, come on. Everyone is talking about it. This isn't a real marriage."

Margo and Chase stopped, stunned. What did she mean? Where they the gossip of the town?

"What?" Chase breathed.

"Everyone is talking about how this is a marriage for money. I didn't believe it at first, but now I see it's obvious. It's sickening. I always thought it was meant to be the woman who is the gold digger, not the man. Well, if you can call yourself that."

Margo jumped to her feet to scold Mrs. Adams, but before any words left her lips, Chase had pushed his chair back so hard it toppled over, and he stormed off in a fit of anger.

CHAPTER 14

hase woke with a throbbing head. Blinking his eyes, he saw bright white lights all around, and the strong smell of disinfectant filled his nose. He turned his aching neck to see Margo asleep, wrapped in a light blanket with mascara tears staining her face. Groaning, he pushed himself to a sitting position. Like a flash of lightning, it hit him. He was in the hospital.

"Margo?...Margo?" Chase groaned; his throat was parched.

Startled, Margo woke, rushing to his side. Relief flooded her face, and fresh tears brimmed her eyes.

"Thank the Lord. Don't move. I'm going to get the nurse," Margo said, running out the door and returning just as quickly.

"What do you remember?" Margo asked. Perching on the edge of the bed, she grasped Chase's hand tightly.

"I remember arguing with Mom...I remember riding off on Harvey and....nothing after that."

"I tried to follow you but caught up just as you galloped out of the barn. You didn't come back all night; we were all so worried. I panicked when Harvey arrived the next afternoon, limping. You were nowhere to be found. I thought the worst," Margo stopped herself, and Chase heard the catch in her voice.

"We went looking for you. We found you in the middle of the woods. You had bashed your head pretty hard on a rock."

"I remember…something spooked Harvey. He went crazy. I couldn't control him, and he threw me. How long have I been here?" Chase asked.

"A month and a half."

Chase felt like he had been slapped in the face. *A month and a half?*

"I thought I was going to lose you," Margo sobbed, tears rolling down her face.

"Lose me?" Chase asked.

Margo froze. Chase sat patiently, holding her hand tight, not wanting to let her go.

"I've been…I have…I've been thinking…." Margo stammered, unable to find the right words.

"I love you too," Chase said.

"What?" Margo gasped.

"I thought I had feelings for you before you leaped to my defense with my mother. I didn't know if you felt the same. We may have been forced into this marriage, but we had something before; who is to say we can't again?"

———

Margo spent the subsequent month nursing Chase back to health. It was a struggle to keep him resting, as the second they got home, he wanted to jump right back into work. Margo had finally made peace with her father and asked him to help with the ranch while Chase recovered.

Before they knew it, the year anniversary of their wedding day approached, which meant only one thing. Should they discuss annulling the marriage? Or would they try and stick it out? But as history likes repeating itself, neither of them wanted to discuss it. After almost losing Chase in a riding accident, Margo realized some things are far more important than deadlines, inheritance, contracts, and money.

Mortality was a fickle thing. And after his accident, Chase vowed not to waste another second of his life. He had spent most of his life keeping people out due to his shaky relationship with his parents. Not anymore. You could say they had a whirlwind romance, but the truth was the feelings had always been there. It had just taken fate to force them together and almost rip them apart for those feelings to come roaring to the surface. It wasn't long after Chase had regained his strength that they finally took the leap and consummated their marriage.

After that, Chase knew how he wanted to spend the rest of his life and how he planned on ending the year-long marriage contract.

———

Margo had ignored the date as much as she could, but time flies. And before she knew it, Christmas was a week away. She didn't want to risk what she and Chase had by bringing up the marriage dead-line. She was scared that if she brought it up, the bubble would burst, that she would wake up and find their romance had been nothing but a flash in the pan – a wonderful dream with a heart-breaking ending.

"Margo? Can we talk?" Chase asked softly, interrupting her thoughts.

"Sure," she answered, closing her laptop.

"I don't think we can avoid talking about it any longer. You know what date it is next week, right?"

"I remember," Margo sighed.

"Well, I don't know where your head is at, but I wanted to ask you something."

Margo felt sick. She feared the worst but firmly believed in ripping the band-aid off.

"Go for it."

"How about we scrap our original plan and renew our wedding vows?"

"What?" Margo gasped, her heart pounding.

"I want to give you the wedding day you always dreamed of. I want you to wear your mother's dress. I want you to stay, Mrs.

Adams....if you will have me," Chase said, all his hope and love shining in his eyes. "So, Margo, will you continue to be my wife?"

Margo knew what she wanted to say. She wanted to scream her answer from the rooftops, but the words that came out of her mouth couldn't be kept a secret for much longer. She had already known for a week. If he was serious, she needed him to know. His reaction would tell her how he truly felt.

"Chase, I'm pregnant."

Chase sat still, unmoving. His face was unreadable before a grin slowly crept across his face.

"If it's a boy, let's name him Harvey."

The End

A HISTORICAL HOLIDAY ROMANCE

The Yuletide Thief

DAISY LANDISH

CHAPTER 1

The clouds quickly rolled over Brighton's smart seafront, revealing darkening streaks of light in the wintry sky. It was time to hurry.

Emily Hawthorne dug her hands deeper into the pockets of her burgundy overcoat as she marched down the promenade. Melting snow slopped in small puddles around her ankle boots. This afternoon's shopping had gone well. She was pleased. There was just one thing remaining on her shopping list now.

A bracing sea breeze coming in from the English Channel whipped at Emily's cheeks, making her cheeks glow with a rosy rue she knew was hardly becoming. Emily loved the sea. Its wildness lured her and filled her fervid imagination with tales of swashbuckling pirates like Blackbeard, Calico Jack, and even Ann Bonney, the infamous woman pirate. These tales, told by her mother, had thrilled Emily as a child and thrilled her still.

Emily had been small for her age. It came from being born before the proper time, the doctors said. Until the age of seven, Emily had had to wear braces on her legs. The awful metal things had been painful, but not as painful as the relentless teasing from the other children she was subjected to because of them. It didn't matter that she was the vicar's daughter. They should have been more Christian to her: the children showed no mercy. Their ringleader had been the magistrate's daughter, Penelope Pendlebury. The years had not seemed to mellow Miss Pendlebury. Though more refined now in her airs and graces, Penelope still appeared to show the same contempt for those less fortunate as she always had.

Emily, on the other hand, was a more compassionate person, largely because of her misfortune. When growing up, she'd become lost in the world of books. Whenever this teasing had occurred, as it often did, dear Mama, upon seeing her so upset, would sit her upon her knee. Then, Mama would read aloud to her stories, stories of princesses and pirates, but mainly stories of pirates. And for a while, Emily would get lost in her mother's warmth and be there in the treasure galleons sailing the Caribbean seas. Emily would forget all her fears and forget that she was a weak cripple for a short while.

Emily was fully well now. Her strength came from all the exercise she did. The doctors had recommended that she walk daily. To this day, she walked outdoors at a vigorous pace that did not always agree with her fair complexion. It was the reason why she marched down the promenade today even though the driver of her carriage, Joseph Arnett, was at her beckoning but a short distance off.

Brighton seafront was busy today. Though cold, many people, like her, hurried to get the last of their Christmas shopping done. Gentlemen tipped their hats at the petite woman marching through their midst. Emily was a fine-looking woman, gold ringlets framing her bonnet. But too small, which is why she thought, she remained unmarried. A poor vicar's daughter, Emily had few prospects but to be a governess or a lady's companion. She loved children, and she would likely make a fair governess. She'd be a fine example to them, just as her mother had been to her; God rest her soul.

If Emily wanted something, she'd set out to get it, and get it she would. Nobody could ever say she was not determined. But the one thing that was not in her power to obtain was a suitable match. Twenty-three and still unmarried, she was almost an old maid. The eligible bachelors were disappearing one by one. And of those that remained only had eyes for Penelope Pendlebury, who was all the things that Emily was not: wealthy, graceful, and tall. Lucky Penelope had all the gentlemen falling at her feet. It wasn't fair. Though she had good looks, she had the personality of an alley cat.

If only I was taller, Emily thought. Then she'd have her pick of the men or at least *some* men. She was sure of it. Though which men, she hadn't quite decided. There was only one man that had ever quickened her heart, the dashing Lord Robert Davenport. But the man was a cad.

Emily hadn't spoken to Lord Davenport since he'd been so rude to her at the church bazaar last summer. She'd been taking a collection for the orphans, and when she'd asked him for a donation, the bounder had laughed right to her face. What he had found so funny, she could not possibly fathom, but Lord Davenport had humiliated her!

Of course, Lord Davenport had tried to speak to her since, but she would have none of it. The man had the arrogance of a peacock. Yes, he may be dashingly handsome, with dark eyes that made her, along with every other woman in Sussex, melt. Though he may have the longest eyelashes she'd ever seen on a man and cut the finest figure in hessian boots and buckskin breeches, he was a bounder! She'd seen him walking out with Penelope Pendlebury. Well, the alley cat was welcome to have him! It was a match made in heaven if she'd ever seen one. Looks fade, but a good heart endures. She preferred to remain unattached than marry a heartless man such as he.

Emily marched across the cobblestones to the bookshop nestling in the shopping arcade across the street. Glittery Christmas baubles twinkled in its windows, their brightness against a darkening afternoon sky reminding Emily that she must get home before night fell. It was an hour's coach ride yet.

Emily pushed open the door to the shop and inhaled the rich aroma of leather-bound tomes full of tales set in lands far away. The adventures called to her like a siren's song. The man behind the shop counter nodded at her. "Good afternoon, Miss."

Emily's jaw tensed. *Miss.* Even the shop assistant presumed a woman as short as she could not possibly be a married lady, let alone a duchess or a countess. Yes, of course, it had to be "Miss". She gritted her teeth and smiled.

"What books have you on pirates?"

CHAPTER 2

Joseph Arnett jiggled the reins as Emily's carriage surged down the country lanes of West Sussex. He kept a good pace, the dappled grey gelding hauling the carriage was a fine, strong animal. Its muscles rippled on its shoulders, keeping them on target to get back home before nightfall.

The carriage heaved with Christmas food and gifts. Spinning tops and dolls poked out of wicker baskets alongside paper hats, crackers, jars of sweetmeats, and children's books. Papa would be so happy. He'd entrusted her with three gold sovereigns, more money than she'd ever seen in her life, to purchase all the items on the shopping list he'd handed to her with a big smile on his face.

Dear Papa, always thinking of others. The orphans would be delighted with their gifts. And then, after they'd seen what Saint Nicholas had brought them this year, they'd tuck into the biggest dinner of their lives that dear Mr. Arnett's homely wife would cook for them all tomorrow.

Emily was so excited. She didn't know how she'd been able to keep the plan such a secret. She was bursting. She'd confided in Mr. Arnett. Heavens, Papa didn't have the means to employ a driver, let alone keep a horse and carriage. The dear man, a long-standing family friend, had volunteered his services to drive her the six miles to and from Brighton for the shopping. He'd even offered to go by himself, but Emily had wanted to make the selection. It felt more personal this way.

The hedgerows in the lane glistened with silver. The water left behind from the slushy snow of earlier started to freeze. It was going to be a cold one tonight. But the last of the afternoon sun glinted on them for now, making everything look beautiful. Jack Frost was working at his finest this Christmas Eve.

Emily looked out at the orange orb of the low winter sun on the horizon and smiled to herself. Snowflakes began to fall gently around her, making the scene even more magical: oh, she loved Christmastime! If only Mama was here to share it. Mama had always made every Christmas special, decorating the vicarage as though celebrating a hundred Christmases at once.

"And why wouldn't I do such a thing to celebrate the Lord Jesus' birth?" she'd say.

The first year without Mama would be so hard to bear for both Emily and her father. The vicarage felt empty without her mother's warm presence, which is why they were going to throw the doors wide open to the orphans this Christmas Day. Emily had long wanted to do something more for the poor children than she already did. This year, she was able to persuade her father to go along with her idea. They'd spoken to the local orphanage, and it was all planned. Everybody was sworn to secrecy, including the Arnetts.

The vicarage that Emily called home was a charming red brick building nestled in the finest of villages in the rolling South Downs that lay to the north of Brighton. Tucked in the prettiest of places, where ducks waddled over from the village pond to the Norman-built church, Emily knew she was blessed to live in such idyllic surroundings. She loved it there; she never, ever wanted to leave. Though she yearned for a husband, she knew she'd be torn to leave it in the event of a marriage. No bachelors were living in the area, aside from the awful Lord Davenport.

As much as she loved this little corner of England, she didn't want to be out it at night, and certainly not on these roads. Besides the apparent dangers of riding in the dark, highwaymen lurked in Devil's Dyke, a deep V-shaped valley on their way home.

But she did not have to worry about that this afternoon. The sky was a glorious orange, which was all the illumination Mr. Arnett needed to get home. And by the time blackness took the sky over, closing another day down, Emily would be already home showing Papa her purchases. They would spend the evening together wrapping gifts and talking about Christmases spent with Mama.

Mr. Arnett's horse entered Devil's Dyke. For a moment, the gelding seemed to hesitate, as if filled with a sense of foreboding, a sixth sense telling it that it must not bide here long lest the devil come out to play. But for now, the place was pretty as a picture. The valley was radiant beneath the low winter sun; the hills were dusted with snow like powdered sugar on a Christmas cake.

Emily sighed with enormous pleasure at the sight. Her reverie was abruptly broken as thundering hooves echoed through the valley. Someone was in a great hurry.

Mr. Arnett, on the reigns, tensed up. Then suddenly, the carriage skid across the gravel to a crunching halt.

"Stand and deliver!"

CHAPTER 3

E mily squinted and saw the silhouette of a man on horseback set against the setting sun. Blocking their way ahead, he held a pistol in Mr. Arnett's direction. Mr. Arnett's hands sprang up.

"Good man," said the highwayman. "I don't want to hurt you." His voice was low, unforgiving, almost a growl.

Mr. Arnett's head bobbed up and down in agreement. The goods on board might be for the orphans, but he had no plans to be a hero. The highwayman gestured with his pistol: *over there.* Mr. Arnett jumped off his perch, went to the side of the road and sat on his hands as directed.

The highwayman leapt off his horse; the massive stallion snorted as if with disgust. The highwayman patted its flank. He was a confident horseman. That much was evident. His muscular thighs in his black breeches further prove that a lean and hard body was on what else.

The stallion's warm breath steamed in the air, and Emily's heart pounded as the highwayman drew nearer. What was he doing out before sundown? Was he that arrogantly assured of his ability to get away?

With the sun no longer in her eyes, Emily could see him better. He was dressed from head to toe in black. A small opening in his mask revealed only the bottom half of his face: a broad slash of a mouth set in a square jaw. Even as Emily trembled, a surge of excitement ran through her core.

He had not seen her yet. Emily shrunk back from the window into her seat. She hardly dared to breathe. She could not see him now but could hear him. His footsteps crunched on the gravel as he slowly walked around the carriage.

"I see someone's been shopping today," he growled, evidently addressing Mr. Arnett.

She heard straps snap back as the goods on top of the carriage were released. The packages made a thud when meeting the ground. Emily winced.

"Does one man need so much?" The highwayman's voice became even lower if that were possible.

"I say one man does..." His boots crunched nearer.

The man rounded the carriage, "... me!"

His voice suddenly trailed off as he saw Emily. His eyes met Emily's. Emily felt a thrill go through her. But he quickly broke eye contact and tipped his three-corner hat at her and threw a calling card into the carriage. What had the world come to if highwaymen had calling cards? Emily picked it up and read: *Robin of Sussex.*

Robin of Sussex was now scooping up the best of the gifts and adding these to his saddlebags. He leapt on his stallion, ready to ride off.

"You should be ashamed of yourself!" exclaimed Emily. "Those gifts were for the orphans."

Robin of Sussex grunted and dug his heels into his horse's flanks. Hooves thundered as the highwayman exited the valley.

But much as Emily detested him for taking the orphans' gifts, she yearned to see Robin of Sussex again. Something was thrilling about the man.

CHAPTER 4

Emily's many petticoats brushed through the snow as she stood by Mr. Arnett's side. It was getting colder now, and the orange orb of the sun had long since gone. The sky was now an inky blue, snowflakes falling fast through it. Only a full moon now illuminated the valley that the devil had laid claim to as his own.

Mr. Arnett's breath was fast and heavy. The gelding heaved as the carriage wheel lurched forward, then sprung back again into the rut. There was no way around it. They were good and proper stuck.

Mr. Arnett shook his head. "Get back on board, Miss Emily, or you'll catch your death. I'll go and fetch help. There's a farmhouse about a half-mile ahead." He nodded westwards as he unharnessed his gelding.

Emily's teeth chattered as she stared in the direction Mr. Arnett pointed. She knew where he meant. She might have gone with him, but she didn't want to leave behind the remaining food and gifts. She'd started fundraising at the church bazaar. The funds collected had been sufficient. If it hadn't been for the anonymous gift of two gold sovereigns pushed through the vicarage letterbox, she wouldn't have gotten nearly as much.

On the whole, Robin of Sussex had taken very little. Emily wondered why. There had been room in his saddlebags.

In addition to the goods for the orphans, there was Mr. Arnett's coach to consider. The man had been good enough to let her have its use. She wouldn't leave for the next bandits to come along.

Robbers and highwaymen were known to roam the valley. A shortcut to London, the aristocracy were known to commute by coach. She presumed Robin of Sussex thought she was one of them in Mr. Arnett's fine carriage.

Emily clambered back on board, took a seat, and nodded gratefully as Mr. Arnett tossed his coachman's blanket to her. His hands went to unbutton his coat.

"No. I can't take that from you, Mr. Arnett. You'll freeze."

He opened his mouth to argue, but Emily's jaw was set firm. There was no arguing with her when she had that look on her face. Mr. Arnett knew her well enough to know that. He'd seen that look of determination on her as a child when she'd made herself walk an extra few yards, even when he knew how much it physically hurt. He'd never known a child so stubborn.

Mr. Arnett nodded; he couldn't pretend he wasn't relieved. It would be cold on that ride to the farmhouse.

"I'll come back with help for you as soon as possible."

Emily nodded and watched him disappear into the darkness, leaving her all alone in the devil's playground.

CHAPTER 5

mily wasn't sure how long she'd been there when she heard fast and furious galloping. The sound of what sounded like a team of a dozen horses echoed through Devil's Dyke.

That was quick! Emily rubbed her eyes and prised open the door of her carriage. The moon lit up the landscape, making it look like the illustration on a Christmas card.

Emily jumped out onto the ground, dusting fresh snowflakes off her coat. She waited as a grand carriage, its lanterns blazing, drew near. It was only then that she realised it came from the east. Mr. Arnett could not possibly send it.

"Woah!" commanded the coachman. The carriage slid to a halt. The team of four horses pawed at the snow, waiting for the signal to go off again.

The coachman tipped his hat at Emily as a tall figure leapt from inside the carriage out into the snow. The man wielded a lantern aloft. It swung back and forth as he approached her. Emily's heart sank when she saw who it was.

"Well, well!" said Lord Davenport.

Of all the people, in all the places, it had to be him! Moonlight illuminated his rugged face framed by dark wavy hair that hinted it tended to be unruly. His brown eyes had a warmth blazing in them that Emily had rarely seen. The most sensual of lips … She stopped herself. She was staring.

His lips curled now into the faintest of smiles.

"What seems to be the trouble, Miss Hawthorne?" he asked. His right cheek twitched. Was he laughing at her?

"Do not make sport of me, Sir!" she snapped.

"Oh, I would never do that, Miss Hawthorne!" He bit his lip, but mirth danced in his eyes at her outrage.

His eyes flicked up and down, giving her the once over. As if he were seeing her for the very first time, he tilted his head to one side and studied her. It made her bristle.

Emily didn't want him to see her like this. She didn't know why she was so vehemently opposed to it, but she didn't. Despite herself, she looked down, looked at what he saw: her wet dress clinging to her slim hips and thighs beneath the petticoats peeped. She wiped a tear of frustration from her eye, then set to straightening her skirts.

"Could I give you a ride, Miss Hawthorne?" Lord Davenport gestured towards the open door of his carriage. It looked warm and welcoming.

Emily straightened another layer of her petticoat. To do so, she had to raise her skirt a little above her ankles to adjust herself. He did not look away as a gentleman should. There was that smirk on his lips again. How dare he!

"No, thank you." Emily shook her head vigorously. "Mr. Arnett is fetching help. *He's* a good man," she gave Lord Davenport a barbed look. "He will be back shortly."

"I cannot leave you here. You'll freeze." Lord Davenport's eyes locked with hers. His expression was earnest, pleading even, Emily fancied.

He waited a moment and saw Emily still shook her head. *No? Was she saying no?* He came nearer. He was too close for comfort. His proximity unnerved her yet made her tingle. Emily noticed her breath was suddenly quicker.

"Are you not aware that highwaymen roam these parts?" He

picked her up and put her over his shoulder. Her petticoats splayed outwards as she kicked in protest.

"A young woman on her own could fall prey to one of those scoundrels—"

He carried her towards his carriage. Emily couldn't believe what was happening. She beat her fists against his back and kicked her feet.

"You're the scoundrel, Sir! Put me down at once!" she shrieked.

Ignoring her protests, Lord Davenport plopped her onto the cushioned seats of his plush carriage. There were several woollen blankets on the seats. It was undoubtedly cosier and warmer than Mr. Arnett's carriage, and Mr. Arnett had a fine carriage.

Lord Davenport spread a blanket out like a knight, spreading a cloak for a lady and placing it on Emily. Several lanterns also blazed in there, generating extra heat. He followed her in and slammed the carriage door shut behind him. He sat opposite her; his eyes locked with hers.

"Well, here we are. You cannot say this is not more comfortable," Lord Davenport said, satisfied with himself.

Emily composed her thoughts. Her fists balled beneath the blanket.

"Mr. Arnett is coming back. If I am not here when he returns, he will worry. I must insist you let me go at once!"

Those eyes were on her, such a deep dark brown. Eyes she could melt into if she allowed herself. She averted her gaze. She was being foolish. He couldn't possibly be interested in her, and besides, he was a cad! She wondered what it was about her tonight. Two men, she was swooning over like some silly young girl. Like Penelope Pendlebury.

"The way I see it, you have a choice." Lord Davenport nodded, counting off the options on his fingers. "One. You stay in your carriage and freeze. I cannot have that on my conscience…."

Emily's eyes went back to meet his, and her heart skipped a beat despite herself. Lord Davenport's gaze stayed on her as he continued. "Or two, you come with me somewhere warm and don't freeze to death. I think that is the better option, don't you…? Don't worry, you are perfectly safe. I'm a gentleman, whatever you think of me."

Emily had not found the words to reply before Lord Davenport banged the carriage roof to signal to his coachman and his team of four horses lunged forward.

"We will, no doubt, meet Mr. Arnett on the way," he added.

"I said Mr. Arnett is coming for me!" Emily stood up, and the blanket Lord Davenport had placed on her with such care dropped to the floor. She swayed with the lurching carriage, trying to steady herself. Her thighs pressed into his knees. Her breasts were too close to his face. It made her uncomfortable and weak all at the same time. She must resist.

She banged the carriage roof.

"Stop! I say stop!"

"Woah!" yelled Lord Davenport.

The carriage slid to a stop again, the force making Emily fall into his lap.

"Or option three, you stay with me here until Mr. Arnett returns."

His warm eyes twinkled, his double-entendre suggesting she remained in his lap! He made no efforts to move her, but she noticed tension now tightened his wide mouth. Emily glared at him. She quickly got up and went back to her seat, straightened herself down. She picked up the blanket again.

"Spoilsport!" he quipped.

Emily maintained her glare, but her heart lurched. His eyes met hers, and she knew he saw that she had felt something while in his lap. It infuriated her to have been so unguarded with her emotions.

"You've forgotten option four, Sir, which is to go back to Mr. Arnett's carriage alone and take my chances."

She sprung open the door of the coach and jumped out… right into the midst of a snowdrift. Her skirts flounced around her as she fought to get back on her feet. There was that laugh again, that deep throaty laugh that had so infuriated her at the bazaar.

"Do not mock me, sir!"

Lord Davenport held out his hand to her. "You wound me, Miss Hawthorne," he said with a pout even as his cheeks twitched with delight.

Once she had taken his hand, he pulled her to him and did not let go of her at once. He held her against his chest. She pushed gently against his shoulders, and he reluctantly let go, or so it seemed to her. She scolded herself for being foolish. It was just wishful thinking on her part. He wasn't interested in her when he had women like Penelope falling at his feet. She met his steady gaze. There was a splash of colour now in his cheeks that hadn't been there before.

She averted her eyes, focusing on anything but the handsome brute before her. The man roused her mind, and her emotions. She felt stirrings within her that she'd never felt before. She frowned at the snowflakes racing by; they were racing like her heart now did in her chest.

Soaked to the bone, Emily knew she must get warm as soon as possible, or she would catch her death. She couldn't do that to Papa when he'd only just lost Mama this year. She must acknowledge the fact she had no choice but to get back into the cad's carriage.

Lord Davenport wrapped her in as many blankets as he could, tucking her up with the care a father would show a sick child. For a fleeting moment, Emily imagined him as a father to her children. No, she must stop this silliness. He was a bounder and already walking out with another lady. Though she had no love for Penelope Pendlebury, she would never interfere in another woman's courtship. And besides... *besides, what*? Emily was quickly forgetting.

"We'll wait here until your Mr. Arnett gets back to secure his carriage." His disconcerting eyes bore into her.

"What happened to you this evening, Miss Hawthorne? Before I came to your rescue, I mean."

Emily sniffed. "We were robbed by Robin of Sussex."

"Robin of Sussex?!" Lord Davenport whistled. "But what were you doing out with Mr. Arnett? Are you related to the man?"

"No. My father and I," Emily stopped, wondering if she should tell Lord Davenport about the orphans. She suddenly remembered why she detested him. Greedy men like him didn't give a fig about the orphans. They only cared about themselves. That's why they were so rich in the first place.

"Your father and you, what?" His eyes were suddenly softer. She hesitated. Why did she suddenly feel compelled to tell Lord Davenport her life story?

"We were doing something for the orphans," she exclaimed. "I'd gone into Brighton with money we'd raised to arrange a proper of Christmas for them."

Lord Davenport nodded.

"But now it's all ruined!" She wiped a furious tear from her eye. She waited for him to mock her, but he didn't.

"And Mr. Arnett's role in this?"

"Mr. Arnett is a kind soul. He and his wife are good Christians. He volunteered his horse and carriage for the venture."

"That was good of him," replied Lord Davenport.

Emily nodded. "Though he is wealthy, Mr. Arnett is charitable. He does not boast of his good works."

Lord Davenport's eyes twinkled at the barb. "But when you do a charitable deed, do not let your left hand know what your right hand is doing, that your charitable deed may be in secret; and your Father who sees in secret will Himself reward you openly." Lord Davenport paused. "Matthew 6:3-5. Mr. Arnett is a prudent man."

Emily looked at Lord Davenport, shocked. Perhaps he was not such a heathen after all. He'd recited the verse with a sincerity that would match any man of the cloth. His eyes met hers, and there was delight at his having disconcerted her so. She was sure this man could read her thoughts.

"It appears Robin of Sussex held you up because he wrongly thought you and Mr. Arnett greedy rich people deserving of being unloaded."

"Indeed, it is a shame you were not before us, Sir, as he should have stopped you instead, and I would not be in this predicament!"

To her surprise, Lord Davenport roared with laughter.

She sneaked a look at him and shyly smiled. Perhaps he was not so bad after all.

Lord Davenport's gaze was steady. "I hear Robin of Sussex is a modern Robin Hood, robbing the rich to give to the poor."

Emily's chin tilted up. "Is that so?"

"Indeed, I've heard tales up and down the counties of orphanages receiving large donations following robberies in the area."

She looked out the windows at the falling snow. Perhaps. The two gold sovereigns suddenly made a lot of sense. Mr. and Mrs. Beaverbrook had been held up but two days before.

She willed herself not to look back at him, for her mind was no longer on the orphans. Her stomach was somersaulting. But Mr. Arnett should be back soon. Then she wouldn't feel this dreadful temptation.

"And you, Sir. What were you doing earlier?" she continued to stare out the window. She had to change the subject.

"Like you, I was shopping."

Emily looked around the carriage. There seemed little on board.

He saw the curious look on her face.

"I was purchasing a gift for Miss Pendlebury."

Emily's nose wrinkled. Then she stopped herself; it wasn't very Christian of her. Penelope must possess some redeeming qualities. Everybody did.

"I'm not sure if I should give it to her now."

What was he saying?

"Why is that Sir?" she asked in a casual tone.

"I may have found a more deserving recipient."

He reached into his breeches pocket and procured a small ring box.

His hand brushed against hers. His voice was husky, emotional. Emily's heart leapt with excitement.

"Open it," he said brusquely.

Emily's head rapidly jerked up. That deep voice, full of danger and promise. It was Robin of Sussex's! Her eyes traced the shape of the same jawline she'd seen illuminated in the orange sunset but two hours before. How could she have been so blind?

"Marry me!"

Emily looked at him and swooned. "Robin!?"

"Robert." Lord Davenport now knelt at her feet. "Stand and deliver your heart to me, Miss Hawthorne."

Emily's heart was already his, and his blazing eyes showed that he knew it.

She nodded, the barest of assents, speechless as he slid the ring on her finger.

Lord Davenport scooped her in his arms, and his lips pressed hard against hers. His kiss was warm and urgent.

"I'm sorry about earlier," he murmured. "I came back for you."

Now that he'd released her mouth, Emily's brain began to churn out several questions.

"But you held Mr. Arnett at gunpoint!" she exclaimed.

Robert reached into his coat and produced the pistol. "It's not real. Look, it's made of wood and stained with coal," he explained, placing it in her hands. Emily gingerly picked up the weapon. It looked accurate enough to her. She turned it on him and asked, "What of this summer? Why did you laugh when I asked for a donation for the orphans?"

"You would make a fine highwaywoman, Emily," he replied with a chuckle. Seeing her steely gaze, he continued. "Because only the day before I had delivered a sizeable 'donation' to the Vicarage."

Emily made to speak, but he pressed a finger against her lips. His voice was still low. "Don't let your left hand know what your right hand is doing."

Emily understood.

In the distance, she heard galloping hooves. Help was on its way. But for now, she didn't mind being stranded in the dark with a highwayman.

The End
Did you enjoy *Mistletoe Magic*?
Please consider rating it on <u>Goodreads</u>, or <u>Bookbub</u>.
Reviews help me reach new readers.

Join my Newsletter at www.daisylandishromance.com for updates, new releases, sales and giveaways!

www.ingramcontent.com/pod-product-compliance
Lightning Source LLC
Chambersburg PA
CBHW022039170626
46808CB00003B/1277